*T*HE *L*ONDON *M*URDER

*M*YSTERIES

Cora Harrison is the author of many successful books for children and adults. She lives on a small farm in the west of Ireland with her husband, her German Shepherd dog called Oscar and a very small white cat called Polly.

Find out more about Cora at:
www.coraharrison.com

To discover why Cora wrote
the London Murder Mysteries, head online to:
www.piccadillypress.co.uk/londonmurdermysteries

The London Murder Mysteries

The Montgomery Murder
The Deadly Fire
Murder on Stage
Death of a Chimney Sweep
The Body in the Fog
Death in the Devil's Den

THE LONDON MURDER MYSTERIES

DEATH IN THE DEVIL'S DEN

CORA HARRISON

PICCADILLY PRESS • LONDON

First published in Great Britain in 2012
by Piccadilly Press Ltd,
5 Castle Road, London NW1 8PR
www.piccadillypress.co.uk

Text copyright © Cora Harrison, 2012

A catalogue record for this book is available
from the British Library

ISBN: 978 1 84812 248 2 (paperback)

1 3 5 7 9 10 8 6 4 2

Printed in the UK by CPI Group (UK) Ltd, Croydon, CR0 4YY
Cover design by Patrick Knowles
Cover illustration by Chris King

This book is dedicated to
Benedict Roberts, aged eight,
who gave me the excellent idea
of sending Alfie up in a hot-air balloon.

CHAPTER 1

THE RENT COLLECTOR

'You find the extra money or you'll all be sleeping on the street next week,' the rent collector growled.

Alfie stared back at him and said nothing.

'Not too nice out there in the freezing fog,' the man went on with a sneer. 'You know the streets of London aren't too safe at the best of times, but they're downright dangerous for them that sleeps rough. That blind brother of yours, the singing bird, someone will get hold of him and put him in a cage when you're not looking. So you just find that shilling and have it ready for me by this time next week. And don't you let that dog of yours snarl at me, neither, or else I'll be feeding him a dose of rat poison.'

Alfie's lips were white as he watched the rent collector turn on his heel and slam the cellar door behind him. He put his arm around Mutsy, smoothing down the rough fur on the dog's back until the growls died away.

He looked around. The cellar in Bow Street was a fairly miserable place – just the one small, damp room where Alfie, his brother Sammy and his two cousins, Jack and Tom, lived, cooked and slept. The rent was far too high already, but so far, in the years since his parents died, Alfie had never failed to scrape the money together to pay it. He would go without food rather than touch the tin box that held the rent money.

But now the tin box was empty.

CHAPTER 2

A DANGEROUS JOB

'What are we going to do?' Alfie asked the question in a low voice. Although, at twelve, he was only a few months older than Jack, Alfie was the leader of the gang, the one that gave the orders. His brother and cousins expected him to know what to do. He didn't meet their eyes but looked instead at Sarah.

Sarah was a good friend of the boys. She worked as a parlour maid at the White Horse Inn and often came to visit them in the afternoon when she was free. She had a sharp brain, so perhaps she could come up with some way of earning money.

But even Sarah was looking blank. She knew as well as he did that, with the air full of choking yellow fog, Londoners with money were rushing to get indoors as fast as possible. No one was going to hang around watching ragged boys performing tricks, and Sammy, a brilliant singer who earned more money than the rest put together, could not sing well in the fog. Sarah herself would not be paid until the end of the month.

Alfie kept stroking Mutsy while his mind frantically searched for solutions.

And then there was the sound of a footstep on the stone steps outside. Someone was coming down to the cellar, moving slowly, pausing from time to time. Someone who was checking that no one had seen him, thought Alfie.

'I'll kill him if he tries to do anything to Mutsy,' whispered Tom hoarsely.

'Shh,' said Alfie, listening intently. The old wooden door to the cellar was worm-eaten and rickety. Every sound travelled through it. The man – and the footsteps were definitely a man's – was very near to them. Alfie imagined that he even heard him draw in a breath.

And then there was a knock.

Not the rent collector's knock – no bang on the door with a stick, no shout to open up. This was a small sound, just two gentle taps with a knuckle.

Alfie took one look around, gestured to Mutsy to stay and went to open the door.

The man wore his coat collar well buttoned up so that his mouth was hidden, and the brim of his hat was pulled down to his eyebrows. Underneath it, Alfie glimpsed a pair of shrewd brown eyes and gasped with surprise.

'Inspector Denham!' he said. 'Come in, sir.'

Inspector Denham stepped quickly in through the door, but he did not speak until Alfie had closed it behind them.

'Good evening, Sarah,' he said with a nod as he removed his hat and unbuttoned his coat collar, 'Sammy, Jack, Tom. Thank you, Mutsy,' he added as Mutsy wagged a welcome. Alfie held his breath. What had brought an important man like Inspector Denham to the cellar? Alfie and his gang had worked for him in the past, but then he had always sent one of his constables to bring Alfie to the police station. He fixed his eyes on the man, while Tom carried over

5

the only chair that they possessed and placed it near the fire.

'I need your help, Alfie,' began the inspector, sitting down. 'I've got a dangerous and difficult job. Someone is passing secrets about a splendid new gun to our enemies, the Russians. We think the spy is a Member of Parliament, one of three MPs who are investigating the new weapon for the War Office. The trouble is we're not sure which of them is the culprit, and we just can't get any evidence. He must know he's being watched and he's covering his tracks.'

Alfie nodded but said nothing and the inspector went on.

'We need to catch the spy passing secrets to his contact. This is where you can help us, Alfie. I'll pay you sixpence a day to watch the MPs and there's a five-pound reward if you find the evidence.'

Sixpence a day! A five-pound reward! Alfie felt a rush of excitement. 'Leave it to me,' he said. 'I'll find the spy.'

'Don't be too confident,' said Inspector Denham. 'This spy has a lot to lose and if he finds you are after him, he'll think nothing of killing you and dropping your body into the Thames.'

Alfie's eyes widened uneasily for a moment, but then he gave a shrug and grinned.

'I'll deliver him to you on a plate of hot toast, if it's the last thing I do.'

CHAPTER 3

A MACHINE FOR KILLING

The bullet whistled through the air and thudded against the wall. And then another and another; again and again with no pause between them.

Alfie gasped as they whizzed below him. This carbine rifle could shoot these newly invented bullets without stopping to reload. An army equipped with guns and ammunition like that would win any war.

Inspector Denham put a finger to his lips and Alfie nodded. He understood the need for stealth.

Alfie and Inspector Denham were in a huge old

building near Leicester Square, in the very heart of London. Hiding in a secret little room at the top of the building, they were looking down at the shooting gallery from a small curtained opening.

Alfie, the spy to catch a spy, Alfie said to himself and grinned with satisfaction. Then he concentrated on watching from his hiding place. Down below were three MPs, and they were all reporting to the government about this new weapon.

'That big one is called Ron Shufflebottom. He's from Yorkshire,' whispered Inspector Denham in Alfie's ear. Alfie nodded, trying not to giggle at the name. Ron Shufflebottom was dressed all in black, rather old-looking clothes. He was a big, tall man with a red face and shrewd eyes. I'd know him again, thought Alfie. Not many men are as tall as that.

'The one next to him is Tom Craddock from Cornwall.' There was a slightly strange note in Inspector Denham's voice, Alfie noticed, and wasn't surprised when the inspector added, 'Scotland Yard suspect him. He's supposed to be a dangerous man, so keep well clear of him.'

Alfie narrowed his eyes, memorising the details. Tom Craddock was not as tall as the Shufflebottom man, but he was above average in height and was wearing a colourful waistcoat of red and blue squares. He had taken the gun from George, the owner of the shooting gallery, and was squinting down the barrel, with one eye closed. After a minute he passed it to the small man beside him.

'Who is the third one?' whispered Alfie.

'That's Roland Valentine from Essex,' said Inspector Denham. 'He's a country man. He has a very big farm there and is supposed to be a great shot. I'd say that he knows more about guns than the other two.'

Roland Valentine was a very thin man with red hair turning white and a long scarf around his scraggy neck. As he tried out the gun, it was clear that he was almost as good at shooting this repeat rifle as the owner of the shooting gallery had been.

Alfie stared at all three men carefully, looking intently at each face. Yes, he would know them again. He moved forward a little, leaning out through the opening, in order to be quite certain.

At that moment Roland Valentine swung the gun and aimed upwards. 'A rat on your ceiling, George!' he shouted. 'Let's see if I can kill it.'

And the bullet whistled past Alfie's nose, missing it by a few inches.

CHAPTER 4

THE
SHADOWS

Alfie shivered. He had been waiting outside the Houses of Parliament in the cold for hours.

Most of the MPs had already come out, taken cabs or walked away. But not the men Alfie was waiting for.

But then, at last, there they were: the three men he had seen in George's Shooting Gallery. They came to a halt under the gas lamp, their backs to a scarlet postbox: Ron Shufflebottom, Tom Craddock and Roland Valentine, who was so handy with a gun and had nearly put an end to Alfie's life. Had he really thought he had seen a rat, or had he seen the face peering down at him and thought he was being spied on? Whichever it was, this man was dangerous.

Alfie could see them quite clearly. Although the air was still foggy, there were no clouds in the sky and a brilliant full moon lit up the whole scene. The three men stood together looking for a cab. So far, Alfie had watched them for three nights, and each night they had shared a cab back to their apartment. Each night Alfie had followed them, running all the way behind the horses, down Whitehall, through Trafalgar Square, and then around to the place where they were staying by the river. But nothing strange had happened.

And it looked as though nothing was going to happen tonight, either. By now, Mr Shufflebottom had succeeded in getting a cab and they were all piling into it, laughing and teasing each other and in a moment the horse was off, its hoofs clattering against the cobbled surface of Whitehall. Alfie gazed after them, too discouraged to follow them for a fourth night.

Inspector Denham had set him up with a newspaper stand so he could watch the suspects and catch the spy. Who would notice Alfie, a ragged, bare-footed, twelve-year-old boy, selling newspapers?

And so, every day, Alfie collected the first editions of the evening papers even before the ink was dry and took his place outside Parliament, and called out 'Paper! Paper! Paper!' in a voice made hoarse by the London fog.

All for nothing, he thought bitterly and turned to go back and join his cousin Tom, who was waiting patiently a few steps away by the newspaper stand.

And then something happened.

A man who had been standing smoking a pipe at the door of St Stephen's Tavern, opposite the Houses of Parliament, emerged from the shadows. He did not even look at Alfie and his bundle of newspapers, but began to cross the road.

This man *was* a spy. Alfie was suddenly quite sure of that. A tall man, with a bushy black beard and a restless head that twisted and turned as his eyes darted here and there. He carried a silver-topped cane and he was wearing a long overcoat made of glossy black fur. His shining silk top hat was placed sideways upon his head and obscured half of his face. The man had been there for a long time, had watched all of the government ministers and backbenchers coming out of Westminster; but unlike them he had not called for a cab. He had stood in the shadows, a tense, alert figure, smoking a cigar and waiting.

Then, when all the others had gone, he had emerged from the doorway, looked from left to right and behind him. He had carefully scanned the road before crossing over and stopping in front of the red postbox. Once again he looked all around him, but Alfie was now facing the railings and was busy tidying his pack of newspapers, carefully matching up their edges.

But from the corner of his eye he could see what the man was doing.

Alfie's eyes were sharp and so were his wits. To a passer-by it would have looked as though the man in the fur coat was just posting a letter; but Alfie was near enough to hear a slight clink of metal and he saw what was happening.

The man was not posting a letter. He was fishing a letter out of the red postbox.

A dark thread had been tied to a heavy key. The man pulled on the key and on the other end of the thread was tied an envelope. The gas lamp shone on it for a few seconds, long enough for Alfie to see the

15

creamy-white of the paper and the red of the sealing wax that kept it tightly closed.

Alfie swallowed hard. By now this strange behaviour, this affair of the hidden letter, had convinced him. This was what he had been waiting for. He had to follow this man, stay with him, but stay unsuspected and unseen if possible.

Alfie had been starting to get very tired of this job. Nothing was happening as far as he could tell. But tonight was different; tonight things were happening at last.

But this man was not one of the MPs. He was not one of the suspects. Alfie glanced over towards the newspaper stand and hoped that his cousin Tom was observing too. He picked one newspaper off the pile and raised it above his head. That was the signal to Tom who stood shivering beside the newspaper stand.

Tom's job was to follow the man first and then, after a while, Alfie would catch up with him and Tom would hang back. In this way they would take turns so that the hunted person would not notice the same boy behind him all of the time. Tom was good at this sort of thing and would be ready as soon as the man in the fur coat began to move. Alfie himself fiddled with his newspapers and tried to think what to do next. Who was this man? And where was he from?

He had come out from the tavern, but he was not the owner, nor was he staying there. Alfie knew everything about St Stephen's Tavern. He had haunted the place for the last four days and knew everyone who worked there and most of the customers who came and went. This man was not from the tavern and yet his shoes were bright and shiny, so he could not have come from far. He had not come by cab either: Alfie had checked every cab that had arrived in the last few hours. Where did he live? He was not the sort of man who would live nearby in Devil's Acre. Devil's Acre was a terrible place, with narrow, stinking streets and tumbledown houses. It was the home of thieves, criminals and people who did not own a penny. There were no respectable houses around. Where had this man come from?

Alfie pondered over the puzzle while he watched the spy from a safe distance.

'Don't let him suspect you,' Inspector Denham had said. 'A dead hero is no good to me. Keep yourself safe. You have your brother and your cousins depending on you. I'll give you sixpence a day for watching and there is a five-pound reward if you lead me to the spy.'

Five pounds, thought Alfie. Five pounds would put to rest all his worries about finding the rent for the cellar. Five pounds would keep the roof over their heads safe for the time being. So he continued to watch.

The next second, the man in the fur coat stripped the thread from the blob of sealing wax, broke the seal, tore open the envelope and put it, the key and the thread into his pocket. He looked quickly at the large folded sheets of paper and they also went into his pocket. Then he looked around once more and held a long, narrow strip of paper up to the gas lamp. He seemed to be reading its words over and over, almost as though he were trying to understand them. Alfie moved a little nearer and saw why the man was puzzled. There on the piece of paper was written in large black capital letters:

**THE QUICK BROWN FOX
JUMPS OVER THE LAZY DOG.**

CHAPTER 5

THE HUNT

What on earth did that mean? Alfie thought furiously as he tidied his newspapers. The whole thing did not make sense.

Then his eyes widened. The man in the fur coat was doing something very strange.

He crumpled up the narrow strip of paper with the strange words on it; but he did not drop it upon the ground, he did not twist it up and put it in his pocket and he did not tear it into tiny strips and toss them into the foggy air.

Instead, he put the strip of paper into his mouth, chewed it and swallowed it down. Alfie was near enough to hear the tiny gulp as the lump passed down the throat on its way to the stomach.

What had been the meaning of that strange sentence? *THE QUICK BROWN FOX JUMPS OVER THE LAZY DOG.*

It had to be something important. Otherwise, why did the man swallow it? But what on earth was the purpose of the message?

I'll talk it over with Sammy, decided Alfie. Sammy had brains.

'Here you, boy! Come here!' The shout echoed through the dark street.

Alfie hesitated and then warily approached. 'Paper!' He forced the word out and waved the midnight edition of the *Daily Telegraph* in front of the man's face. A strange face, he thought, forgetting his fear in the excitement of the chase. He was near enough now to see what lay behind that side-tilted top hat. One side of the man's face was ordinary: watery eye, reddish cheekbone, heavy moustache and beard; but the other side was terribly scarred, the lip puckered and, eerily, no hair grew from either moustache or beard on that half of the face. What a strange face for a spy, Alfie thought, the sort of face that no one could help but remember. It certainly wasn't any of the men that Inspector Denham had shown him.

Alfie's eyes went to the man's pocket. The contents of the envelope made a slight bulge there. Alfie was an accomplished pickpocket. Would it be possible for him to slip it out without the man noticing? Still, that was not what Inspector Denham was paying him for. His instructions were clear. Follow the man; see where he goes; if possible find out where he lives.

'Paper, sir?' he asked again. 'There's a 'orrible murder on page three, sir, read all about it.'

The man held out a gloved hand and dropped a penny into Alfie's outstretched palm. Alfie handed over the *Daily Telegraph*.

And without reading it or even glancing at it, the man thrust the paper into the other pocket of his fur coat and began to walk briskly down towards Whitehall.

Alfie dropped back and saw with satisfaction that Tom was already following the spy. He was going to have to dump his papers. The man had the opportunity to have a good look at his face while he was buying the newspaper. Alfie abandoned the *Daily Telegraphs* without a moment's qualm. They might not be there when he got back, but he wasn't going to worry about it. Soon he might be the owner of that five pounds!

Alfie seized a broom, smeared some liquid mud from a puddle over his face and then followed at a safe distance. Alfie the newspaper boy had outlived his usefulness – now Alfie the road sweeper would have to take his place.

By the time Alfie overtook Tom, the man in the fur coat had reached Trafalgar Square and was heading towards Pall Mall.

'Never looked once at me,' murmured Tom as Alfie passed him. 'But he was a bit nervous-like when he saw a policeman and he crossed over the road to get away from him.'

Alfie made no sound and did not even look at his cousin. Tom and he had played this game before and both were good actors. Tom was crying 'Paper, paper!' now and had turned towards Whitcomb Street. Alfie followed the spy, keeping a safe distance, hoisting his broom over his shoulder and strolling along, glancing from side to side, but never once looking at the man ahead. Occasionally 'Old-fur-coat', as he nicknamed him in his mind, glared over his shoulder, but he didn't even seem to see the road sweeper. Boys like Alfie were almost invisible in the London streets.

Five minutes later, Tom was in front, and Alfie saw how he was taken by surprise when the man turned suddenly into Albemarle Street. Tom stopped too abruptly, swivelled around too fast and crossed the road when it was clear, allowing himself to be seen under a gas lamp.

'Hey!' There was a note of suspicion in the voice of the man with the fur coat. Alfie flattened himself into a doorway and watched. Tom was doing the right thing. He had crossed the road again and was looking into a shop window as if he had no interest in the man.

Alfie stayed where he was. The street was empty and the man was suspicious. Tom had definitely been spotted. He would have to go home.

Now it was all up to Alfie.

But then the luck changed for the better. A large group of well-dressed men came out of Brown's Hotel and headed towards New Bond Street, talking and laughing loudly. The spy lingered and then walked close to them. Now he was almost hidden by the drunken set, but so, too, was Alfie, darting from doorway to doorway, always ready to fade into the shadows if the man looked around once more.

But he didn't. He walked quickly and confidently until he left the crowd of merrymakers at the next junction.

There was a different air about him, Alfie thought. He strode rapidly and purposefully up the street with the appearance of someone who knows where he is going and what he must do.

Alfie followed cautiously until he reached the broad trunk of a plane tree and leaned against its scaly bark feeling thankful that the nearest gas lamp was well away from him, beside the building where the man had stopped.

Old-fur-coat didn't stand on the pavement for long. He took one glance around, saw that no one was in the street and then went quickly up the steps. He pulled the papers from his coat pocket, wrapped them in the newspaper and pushed the copy of the *Daily Telegraph* into the letterbox, tapped on the knocker, turned and went back down the steps, crossed the road and stood in the shadows of another doorway.

Alfie smiled to himself. There was a big brass plate fastened to the door where the man had posted his copy of the *Daily Telegraph*. The light from the gas lamp shone on it and he could read the letters clearly. One line meant nothing to him, just squiggles, but underneath it in ordinary capitals he saw: *The Russian Embassy.*

And then the door to the Russian Embassy opened. A man, wearing a white silk evening scarf over his coat and an opera hat on his head, came out of the door and looked up and down the pavement. He was smoking a cigar and the smell of it was unusual, almost perfumed. He began to walk slowly, still smoking, the scent of his cigar drifting in front of him. His eyes rested for a moment on the man in the fur overcoat, and then moved away from him. He yawned, stretched his arms high above his head, the cigar still between his fingers, then strolled across the road to a small garden with an iron railing all around it.

Without going in, the man from the Russian Embassy took something from his pocket, leaned over the railing and put a small package, wrapped in brown paper and tied with string, on to an iron bench just inside the railing. Then he yawned again, puffed a little more on his cigar, crossed back over the road, mounted the steps and re-entered the Russian Embassy.

Nothing happened for a moment.

Alfie held his breath and squeezed himself against the tree trunk.

And then the man in the fur coat, who Alfie was sure by now was the spy from Westminster, walked over quickly. He picked up the small package, thrust it into his pocket and turned back in the direction of Alfie's tree.

CHAPTER 6

SUSPICION

The spy was within a foot of the tree, and Alfie was prepared to run, when there was a creaking noise from above. A light was switched on in the upstairs window of the house opposite the tree and the window was flung open.

'Look at that moon!' said a woman's voice from above and then it was joined by a man's voice murmuring something. Alfie let his breath out in a gentle sigh of relief. The spy in the fur coat glanced upwards and began to walk briskly away. Alfie stayed very still and waited until the window had been closed again and the curtains drawn over it.

Then he darted out from behind the tree. Keeping well into the shadows, he went in pursuit.

The man was easy to follow now. Alfie was prepared for the route and, by the time they were going down Whitehall, he grew careless. He was dead tired and could not stop himself yawning. Only one more thing remained for him to do, and that was to find out where the spy in the fur coat lived – and if possible, to get his name. Then, in a few hours' time, when Bow Street Police Station opened for the day, he could make his report to Inspector Denham. Alfie spotted an abandoned meat pie on a bench, picked it up and crunched into the hard pastry. It was deliciously full of gravy with little pieces of steak and kidney inside it and it put new energy into him. Soon the long night would be over. This man must live somewhere near.

But was that really the only thing he could do, he asked himself as they reached Westminster Abbey. The pie had given him courage. After all, he was a practised pickpocket. Surely he could take the brown paper package from the spy's overcoat pocket?

Inspector Denham would be delighted to get it and Alfie himself was very curious to know what was inside the small square parcel.

Alfie fumbled in his own pocket and picked out a penny. It was a bright new penny and, seen in the dim light of the candle-lit window of Westminster Abbey, it could pass for a half-crown. In a second he was beside the man, holding out the penny and saying in an angelic tone of voice:

'Beg your pardon, sir, you dropped this, sir.'

At the same time, his other hand slid into the wide entrance of the fur-coat pocket.

It did not work, though. The man hardly glanced at the penny, but instantly felt the threat to his parcel. A hand like a bone crusher gripped Alfie's wrist and twisted it mercilessly.

And the other hand produced something long and pointed from a concealed pocket inside the stout leather boots.

Within one inch of Alfie's neck was the long, wickedly sharp blade of a knife.

Could he escape? Alfie looked around wildly, struggling silently against the grip on his wrist, digging his nails into the man's soft palm and lowering his teeth towards the hand.

All around him were stately buildings, places for the rich: the Houses of Parliament, its newly-cut stone shining white through the fog; smoke-blackened Westminster Abbey and Westminster School; all huge, magnificent buildings, splendidly ornamented with carved towers and statues.

But only a few yards away from this splendour lay Devil's Acre – that den of the devil, that terrible place of narrow streets filled with rotting houses, of blind alleys where the smell hit you as you approached, and of small square courts with houses crowded around a central space where the filth was heaped as high as the houses themselves. Devil's Acre was a place where thieves, cracksmen and murderers lived side-by-side with the poor and the starving. It was not a place where a well-dressed gentleman in a fur coat, a silk top hat and a silver-topped cane would willingly go.

Alfie made a sudden lunge, broke free and sprinted in that direction. He knew Devil's Acre well. There were no gas lamps there, just a few pitch torches burning outside the inn. He could lose himself easily there.

But he was too late. The silver-topped cane was thrust between his bare legs and he fell heavily to the ground. The fall winded him badly. There was no way that he could escape. He lay gasping for breath.

The wickedly sharp knife flashed as it descended towards him. Alfie abandoned all hope and shut his eyes. This was it.

CHAPTER 7

REFUGE

Suddenly, there was a sound. Something flew through the air. As Alfie lay on the road, gasping like a stranded fish, he saw the black silk top hat spin from the man's head and land in the gutter. Beside it lay a small lump of yellow stone. The man hesitated and looked around behind him. The light from the gas lamp illuminated the terrible scar on his face. He looked up towards the roof of the abbey and then something else came whizzing down and struck the cobbled pavement at his feet.

The man cursed. Alfie had heard most curses, but this one was not known to him. It sounded like some strange language, he thought, as he watched the man pick up his hat and begin to run. But as he did so, another missile came flying down and struck him on the back of the head.

This time he stopped and looked back. The light from the gas lamp showed nothing but a hard, green pea lying on the ground. The strange mouth, half-bearded, half-naked, twisted into an evil grin. He raised the knife and came back, barring Alfie's escape path. He bent down, so near that Alfie could smell a strong smell of tobacco from him. The eyes, he thought, were the eyes of a madman. He shut his own. There was no way that he could escape that wicked knife. All was over with him. He had nowhere to go to escape this man.

And then a chance!

Bullets of hard peas were raining down, shot from the porch roof. They stung the man's face and Alfie heard him swear – again in that strange language. The man straightened himself and took a step towards the Abbey and away from Alfie. Gazing upwards, he shouted 'Who's there?' in a threatening voice.

A different voice whispered urgently to Alfie. 'Up here!' It appeared to come from the roof of the Abbey. 'Here, climb up by the door.'

Alfie was on his feet instantly. He jabbed his fist straight into the centre of the large stomach so near to him and, almost before the words were finished, placed his foot on the first piece of carving that decorated the small door at the side of the Abbey.

When he was halfway up, he risked a glance over his shoulder. The scarred man had moved closer to the door, out of the range of the shooter on the roof. He must have realised that he had been hit by peas and that he just had a pair of boys to deal with. But the strange thing was that after that first exclamation he made no further sound, did not call out, did not threaten – did not behave as most adults would when shot at by a boy.

And, even stranger, he did not attempt to call to the policeman who had just come into sight and was parading past the Houses of Parliament, swinging his truncheon in one hand and fiddling with his whistle with his other hand.

He's the spy, all right, thought Alfie as he climbed. Any honest man would have called the policeman's attention to the person on the roof, would have complained that someone had flung a piece of stone and then shot peas at him from a peashooter. It was probably breaking some law to climb up to the roof of the Abbey, but Alfie didn't care. The man had put his knife away, but Alfie remembered how sharp it had been and how long the blade was and how it had glinted under the light of the gas lamp.

'There's a rope just above your hands,' came the whisper. 'Grab onto it and feel for footholds with your feet. He's still there. He's just waiting for you to come down again.'

Alfie did what he was told. Big Ben, the new clock at Westminster, struck twelve as he climbed, startling him for a moment. Like most Londoners, Alfie was still not used to that giant bell with its booming sound. Then he took a firmer grip on the rope and found that the stone was pitted in places and his bare toes could get a good grip. The voice of his friend on the roof belonged to a toff; but what was a toff doing on top of Westminster Abbey roof? Sometimes, during the day, men with ladders came and repaired something, but no one in their sane senses would be up there on a winter's night.

'The rope finishes there,' whispered the voice with the swell's accent. 'Grab the devil's head and pull yourself up by it.'

An ugly, leering, carved face peered down with water dripping from it. It was green and slimy but Alfie managed to get a firm grip onto the stone curls and lever himself up. In a moment he was on a small, narrow section of roof above the door. The light was dim here, but it was enough to show that the voice that had guided him up belonged to a boy no older than himself.

'Keep still for a minute,' whispered the voice. 'He's going away.'

Alfie's heart beat with relief. Perhaps the man was going to give up the chase.

'Where's he going?' he whispered back.

'Into Little Dean's Yard.'

By now Alfie could see his rescuer more clearly. He was a boy of about Alfie's own age and size, but not dressed in rags as Alfie was. This boy wore a suit like a gentleman and his shirt, though stained with smears of mud and streaks of wet moss, had been stiffly starched and the points on his collar still stood up beside his chin. He had a well-combed head of blond curls and a pair of blue eyes. He must be one of those posh schoolboys from Westminster School, thought Alfie.

'I'm Richard,' he said, holding out a hand that had a few smudges of dirt on it, but felt soft – the hand of a boy who had never had to work. 'What's your name?' he asked politely.

'Alfie . . . I'd better be getting out of here. Will you be safe?' Alfie looked anxiously at the young gentleman who had probably saved his life. Young gentlemen, in his experience, knew little about the rough underbelly of London. Richard wouldn't know what it was like to be hunted through the streets or across the rooftops of the city. It would be just a game to him. 'That fella's got a knife,' he added.

The boy, however, seemed quite unworried and continued to study Alfie with a smile, until a slight sound from below made him peer down at the pavement.

'He's coming after you. What a lark,' said Richard with a chuckle. He leaned over the parapet and peered down. 'Found himself a ladder, too! I wonder how he managed to get hold of that? It's kept in the gardener's shed at the back of the yard. How would he know about that? And how did he get a key to go into the yard? It's always locked at night.'

Alfie joined him and peered over the edge of the parapet; but Richard suddenly drew well back.

'Oh my sainted aunt,' he said under his breath. 'I know who that is. I can't be wrong. I know those hunched-up shoulders – I should do. I spend enough hours staring at them while we're rehearsing in the Abbey. He's disguised himself, though. He doesn't really have a beard, or a scar, or those bushy eyebrows. He must be wearing some sort of mask.'

'Who is it?' asked Alfie in a whisper.

'Boris Ivanov, the organ master at the choir school. I'd stake a penny on it. Never seen that fur coat before, but I'm sure that it is he. I'm in terrible trouble if he finds me on the roof in the middle of the night. He'll flog me if he catches me.'

'He'll certainly kill me,' whispered Alfie back; but his heart was beating hard with excitement as he followed Richard along a gulley that lay between two sections of the roof.

'Boris Ivanov . . .' Alfie tried the words on his tongue. 'Sounds funny!'

'Oh, he's Russian,' Richard replied.

Alfie's eyes widened. What was it Inspector Denham had said?

'. . .*passing secrets and plans about a new weapon, a splendid new gun, to our enemies, the Russians.*'

And the man had been to the Russian Embassy. Things were starting to fall into place!

CHAPTER 8

SANCTUARY
FOR ALFIE

'Yes, he's a Russian. He's always talking about Russia; tells us that he had no parents, no brothers or sisters – just Mother Russia,' whispered Richard over his shoulder as he led the way. 'Funny old cove – great musician, though. You should hear him play the organ. Be careful here, this roof is very slippery.'

'Anything the matter, sir?' The voice rang out clearly in the foggy air.

Alfie groaned to himself as Richard muttered, 'The copper! Now we're in trouble. Edge up here;

careful of that gutter – it's broken. Don't put any weight on it. Get behind this chimney.'

Alfie did what he was told. His bare feet were proving to be more useful than Richard's gleaming black leather boots.

And then the shrill note of a policeman's whistle split the air and Richard moaned. 'That's torn it. The coppers will surround the Abbey. Quick, follow me. Boris will have some explaining to do and that will give us a few minutes' start on them.'

'It's a boy, a boy selling newspapers, stole my purse.' The Russian organist sounded flustered.

Alfie clambered over the head of a stone lion and crouched down beside Richard, whose white teeth flashed a grin in the moonlight. A cool customer, thought Alfie admiringly.

'That boy over there?' asked the policeman. 'Come back, you young villain; come back, I say!'

The policeman was shouting at another boy, down below, and Alfie recognised Tom! He realised that his cousin must have come back to Westminster, instead of going back to the cellar in Bow Street. So now Tom was making a run for it – and, knowing Tom, he would be trying to take the newspapers with him.

Alfie's heart lurched. Tom could be annoying, but Alfie's mother had been very fond of him and she had told her son to look after his cousin when she died. He imagined her above in the heaven of his grandfather's tales and he winced as a picture of her reproachful face flashed in front of his mind's eye.

You were always a troublemaker, he could hear her say. *And now you've got your little cousin into trouble.*

I'm doing my best! The words were in his mind, but they didn't help. He would feel guilty for ever if Tom was caught and dragged off to Newgate prison. The penalty for stealing a gentleman's purse could be death by hanging.

'Good,' said Richard calmly, breaking into Alfie's thoughts. 'They've found someone to occupy them. Careful here; grab onto that saint's hand. Put your foot on his foot. It's quite firm. I've been up here hundreds of times.'

Alfie did as he was told, fitting his bare toes around the carved stone beneath the statue's feet and then stepping up onto the foot itself. The voices of several policemen moved nearer. Had they given up on the chase after Tom? They seemed to be talking to the Russian now.

'Come down from that ladder, sir, if you please. It's an offence to scale a building like the Abbey.' The constable's voice was polite: the man was obviously a toff, wearing a fur coat and a silk top hat, but there was no doubt that he was behaving suspiciously.

'This is a tricky bit,' whispered Richard. 'We have to make a jump here. Don't look down.'

Alfie's mouth was dry as he watched the boy, hand on hat, coat tails flying up, make a leap from the roof to a wall. For a moment it looked as though he would fall, but at the last moment he recovered his balance.

'Come on,' Richard said quietly. 'You can't go back down there. The place is swarming with policemen. They're always around when the MPs sit late. They fetch cabs for them and things like that.'

Alfie knew that he shouldn't go back down for a while until the policemen had wandered off back to New Scotland Yard. Left to himself, he would have spent a few hours on the Abbey roof and then climbed down around dawn. Once more he glanced down at the distance that Richard had leaped so effortlessly. It must be at least thirty feet above the ground, he thought, feeling his breath shorten. He imagined what a fall would do to him, pictured himself splayed out on the pavement with his skull split and the blood oozing from him, like that steeplejack he had once seen fall from the roof of St Martin's church in Trafalgar Square.

From the other side of the Abbey, he could hear more voices and the strong Russian accent of the organist as he tried to explain to the policemen why he had been starting to climb onto the roof of Westminster Abbey in the middle of a winter's night.

'Don't look down – look at me. Jump!' Richard's voice had a note of alarm in it. He could see something that Alfie could not.

And then one policeman's voice rose up, stronger and louder than the others.

'You just stay down here, sir,' it said. 'Constable Davies will get him. 'e's from Wales – 'e's used to mountain climbing and 'e's younger than you are, begging your pardon, sir. He'll catch the little beggar what stole your purse, sir.'

That settled it. A young, fit, mountain-climbing Welshman, armed with a truncheon, was after him. He had to trust Richard. After all, he told himself desperately, Alfie Sykes could do anything that a boy dressed in a tailcoat and wearing a hat and a pair of boots could do.

The distance between the two buildings was only about four feet. That was not the problem; it was just that it was a very long way down if he happened to jump short. However, Alfie's mind was made up. Clamping his teeth tightly together and pulling a deep breath into his chest, Alfie leaped across, clawing at the wall's parapet with stone-cold hands. For a moment he fumbled, but then despair sent the blood flowing back into his veins and he felt the slightly rough surface through his fingertips.

Richard did not say a word but slipped around a pillar and began to scramble up the slippery slate roof of a building joined to the wall. This was more difficult than the Abbey's roof, but Richard twitched a rope and Alfie grabbed hold of it instantly. Quickly they came to a set of tall chimneys, hot to the touch and still smoking slightly. Once behind them, Alfie sighed with relief.

They were no longer on the Abbey roof but on a building close by. Alfie looked down and saw the small yard that Richard had spoken of – Little Dean's

Yard, he had called it. It was shaped like a square, paved in two colours of soot-stained stone and was surrounded by tall, neat brick buildings on all sides. What took Alfie's attention, though, was the archway. There was a stout wooden gate with heavy bars on it, blocking it at the moment; but he was sure that it would be opened when morning came and that he could get out through there and back into Westminster again. In the meantime, he would just follow his new friend along the narrow crest of the roof.

Richard was lying down now, seeming to squash himself against the roof ridge, a hand on the slope on either side. It was a good precaution as the sky was still unclouded and watery gleams of moonlight seeped through the fog. There was a danger that anyone looking out of one of the buildings opposite might see them. Eventually they came to another of the tall chimneys and, with a sigh of relief, Alfie was able to follow Richard's example and to straighten himself against its bulk.

'Don't slip,' whispered Richard. 'I did once and I only saved my life by grabbing onto that flagpole down there by the gutter. It was a near thing, I can tell you. I tied the rope onto the chimney after that.'

Alfie looked down. The roof was a steep one and the fog-wet slates were incredibly slippery. More than ever he admired the nerve and courage of this Westminster schoolboy.

'In here!' Richard pushed open a casement window to the back of the chimney. He climbed over the windowsill into a small dark room. 'This is my study. I share it with Smith Minor, but he's been sent home with measles. You can sleep there and, in the morning, I'll bring you breakfast. Here's a box of matches if you want to find your way around. I'll draw the curtains. Better go now before I'm missed from the dormitory. I'll be flogged to death if I'm found out.'

As soon as he was gone, Alfie lit a match, looked around rapidly, noting the position of the furniture and the cupboards, and then blew it out. Darkness was safer. He felt his way around and took a cushion from a chair and made himself a bed inside a large cupboard whose shelves were full of old books. Once he was settled there, he pulled the door almost shut. Now, if anyone chanced to look in before Richard came, there would be nothing to be seen. He determined not to move unless all was safe.

Richard would be in trouble from the school authorities if they found out about his night on the roof of Westminster Abbey; but if Alfie were found by the Russian spy, it would be a matter of life or death.

CHAPTER 9

THE TOFF

It was a long night for Alfie, stuck in an airless cupboard and listening to every sound. There were noises of mice – or at least he hoped it was mice, not rats – running up and down the wooden panelling behind his head. He tapped on it once and it felt hollow and a piece of board fell out across his knees.

Cautiously he lit a match. Inside the cupboard there was little chance of the light being seen by anyone. There was an empty space behind the board, and beyond that a rough brick wall crossed by horizontal wooden beams. Carefully, Alfie worked a second board loose and then held up another burning match, peering into the darkness above. Using the horizontal beams as a ladder, Alfie climbed up. There was some sort of storage space above. Alfie came out into it and realised that he was in a large, bare attic. He could see cobweb-festooned trunks, suitcases, tuck-boxes and bags lined up there. And then came more scuttling sounds. Hastily he climbed back down, returned the two boards to their rusty nails and tried to sleep.

'Alfie!' The voice was quiet, not much more than a whisper, but it woke Alfie instantly. He waited for a second, but when his name was repeated he was certain that it was Richard. He pulled open the door and peered out.

'Breakfast?' He lifted his eyebrows enquiringly, his voice cool and undisturbed. The last thing he wanted to happen was for Richard to guess how lonely and scared he had been through the night.

'I've got to go to choir practice first.' Richard quickly pulled a black gown over his suit and wondered aloud where he had left his 'lid', eventually finding a flat hat, shaped like a square with a cap beneath it.

'So that's a lid,' said Alfie with a grin. 'Looks funny.'

'It's called a mortarboard, really.' Richard sounded a little annoyed and Alfie suppressed the grin and said that perhaps he should leave while the boys were at choir practice.

'I say,' said Richard. 'I've thought of something. Smith Minor has left his second set of togs here. Why don't you put them on while I'm at the Abbey? It'll make it much easier to smuggle you out when morning school is over. Luckily it's Friday. We have a half-day on Friday and only one choir practice. You might as well stay until then and I'll go out with you – piece of cake, really. No risk.'

He pulled out a suit of clothes from the tall cupboard, found some underclothes and a stiffly starched white shirt in the drawers of a tall chest and a pair of boots from a chest beside the fireplace.

'Light the fire, like a good fellow; I'm late!' And then he was gone. Alfie turned the key in the lock and stood by the door for a few minutes, listening to the sounds of boys' feet clattering down the staircase.

Would he like a life like this? he wondered as he scrunched up bits of newspaper and put some sticks into the fire, adding small pieces of coal once it began to burn freely.

These young gentlemen had everything provided for them, he thought and looked admiringly around at what Richard had called 'his study'. There were two easy chairs by the fire, two desks and chairs on either side of the window that opened onto the sloping slated roof. There was a hook above the fireplace where a kettle could hang, a shelf full of books, a carpet on the floor, a clock, and even a mirror hanging over the fireplace.

Alfie filled the kettle from a tall jug on a side table, set it above the flames and then studied himself in the mirror. He looked very dirty, he thought, and resolved to wash before putting on Smith Minor's spotless shirt. There were some bars of strong-smelling soap and plenty of torn-up rags in the chest and he washed carefully, even his hair, before dressing himself in the starched shirt and black suit of clothes. The well-polished boots were a little too big, but that was just as well because, like every winter, Alfie's toes were swollen by chilblains.

'He was there – there in the abbey as usual!' Richard had scratched gently at the door when he arrived back and Alfie had been pleased to see him. 'I say, what a lark! You look quite like Smith Minor, too. He has black curly hair just like you. Wears it a bit shorter, though. Hang on, let me put the cheese and bread over on the table and then I'll snip it a bit for you.'

'Who was there?' asked Alfie as Richard made the tea in a round brown pot.

'Boris! Mr Ivanov. The organist. He was in a foul mood, too. Kept quarrelling with Mr Ffoulkes, the choirmaster. They're usually the best of friends; but today the pair of them were so bad-tempered with each other that we all escaped. No one got beaten this morning. I even sang a false note and got away with it! Anyway, tell me what you were doing in Westminster last night. Why was Boris chasing you?'

Why would a man who has a good job like an organist want to be a spy? Alfie wondered about that. Normally he would have kept his information to himself, but Richard had, after all, saved his life. As he began to tell the whole story, he pushed away the thought that he was trying to impress this young toff.

'A spy!' breathed Richard when Alfie had finished. 'I say, what a lark! It's like a book. I'm not surprised though. He's crazy about Russia. We all keep muttering, *Why don't you go back there, then?* But now I know why he doesn't. He's spying for his precious Mother Russia.'

'That's it,' said Alfie with satisfaction. It was good to understand. That was why the organist was taking all those risks. He took another big bite of the bread and cheese and washed it down with some tea. He had never tasted tea before; it was too expensive for him and his gang. He decided that he didn't like it that much. Beer was better, he thought, but drank the tea politely.

'Can I help you?' asked Richard eagerly. 'Between us we'll catch him. We need evidence, though.'

'He had papers on him,' Alfie said, 'the drawings of the new rifle and of the special bullet, I'd say. I don't have any evidence – he gave them away. But he did get something in return. He had it in his pocket last night.' And then he told Richard how Boris had eaten the note and posted the papers within a newspaper into the letterbox of the Russian Embassy and how a small package had been left for him to pick up.

'If I could get into his room . . .'

'I must be off!' Richard suddenly looked at the clock on the mantelpiece with alarm. 'Stay here until I get back,' he hissed and then he was gone.

Alfie locked the door behind him and settled down to do some hard thinking. He could go to Inspector Denham with his suspicions, but how much better to have hard evidence! He had not actually seen the piece of paper that Boris had put in his pocket. Could they have been drawings of the invention? But there was the package that he had got in return and put into his coat pocket. With Richard as a witness, or better still, if he could manage to smuggle the package into Inspector Denham's office that would definitely be proof. Then he could claim his five pounds' reward for finding the spy who was betraying England and giving away its secrets.

CHAPTER 9

THE DARK CLOISTER

'Quick, all the seniors are coming down the stairs now! They won't notice you. They never look at us juniors.' Richard burst into the room as soon as Alfie had unlocked the door, gave him a quick look, brushed down the coat, straightened the necktie and then pushed him out onto the landing while he relocked the study door.

Alfie took a deep breath. He would have found it easier to climb back out of the window and along the roof ridge towards the Abbey, than to brave the crowd of boys pouring down the stairs from their studies.

They looked more like men than boys and it seemed strange to think that they were still at school. However, they were inky around the fingers and they wore the same necktie as Richard and he wore. Their deep, or half-broken, voices filled the stairwell with a sound like thunder. They took no notice of the two twelve-year-olds, but pushed past them as if they did not exist.

Richard said nothing and Alfie was thankful for that. As soon as he, with his London accent, opened his mouth they would know him for a stranger, but while he kept silent he was safe.

'Quietly, boys, please!' A tall man, wearing a flowing gown and a mortarboard, came out of a room on the ground floor and looked up. He was followed by a familiar figure: Boris, the organist, an ordinary-looking man with a square, heavy-featured face, now that he was no longer wearing the mask that he had put on last night. Alfie gulped hard and looked down at his boots.

'Sorry, Mr Ffoulkes,' said one of the oldest boys, while another, treading heavily on Alfie's chilblains, muttered to his friends, 'Who does he think he is, blasted choirmaster – he's got no authority over us.'

Richard nudged Alfie and together they slid behind the backs of two heavily built boys. Richard turned the handle of the door and, in a moment, they were alone.

'This is the Dark Cloister. It leads straight into the Abbey,' said Richard. 'The choir always goes down this way and I'm one of the choir so nobody can question me – I'll say that I've left my hymn book in the choir stalls.'

Richard led the way. Alfie could see why it was called the Dark Cloister; it was black as pitch and without Richard's grip on his arm he would have stumbled. He was glad when they came into the dim light of the Abbey and made their way to the choir stalls. No one else was there.

'Let's sit here for a few minutes and we can talk,' said Richard as he sank down on a bench at the very back row of the stalls.

Alfie looked around. It was a good place to talk because each of the benches had a carved kneeler in front of it and these rose so high that they almost completely hid the boys from sight. In any case, the Abbey was very dark, with just a pinprick of light coming from a red lamp on the altar.

'I've got an idea and it's a jolly decent one,' announced Richard. 'I thought I could search old Boris's room and get the evidence. The only thing is, the only safe time to do that is when he's playing the organ here in the church. He'll be playing tonight for Evensong service.'

'I'll go with you,' said Alfie resolutely. He was the one who should get that fur coat with the evidence. He was determined about that.

'Well, I don't think that is possible,' said Richard. 'You see I'll need you to take my place in choir. Old Ffoulkes is as blind as a bat, but he does count heads. If there aren't sixteen heads sticking up from the stalls, he'll go raving mad and not rest until he discovers who is missing. He's got a very nasty temper and it will mean a first-class beating for me if he catches me missing evensong.'

'Well, I can't sing a note and my hair is black and yours is blond,' pointed out Alfie.

'Yeah, it mightn't work. He's probably more likely to miss a voice than to notice about hair colour,' said Richard thoughtfully. 'Especially as I'm the best treble in the choir; he'd probably miss me.'

'I've an idea.' Alfie's voice rose with excitement

and quickly he hushed it. 'My brother Sammy is a great singer – he has a really high voice – and he has hair just like yours. We could dress him up in these clothes. He's nearly as big as I am, so they'd fit him well.'

'That's the solution, then,' said Richard triumphantly. 'Let's go and get him. We've plenty of time. As long as we are in our places before evensong starts, we've nothing to do this afternoon.'

'There's only one problem, though,' said Alfie slowly. 'My brother is blind.'

Sammy had not been born blind, but when he was about two years old he had been very ill with the spotted fever. When he recovered, it was obvious that he had no sight left. The boys' grandfather was a gifted musician and fiddle player and he had worked with Sammy and taught him to sing hundreds of songs.

He has a golden voice, their grandfather used to say to his daughter when she worried about her son's blindness. *It will see him through life, don't you fret.* Now Alfie and Sammy's mother was long dead, and Sammy sang on the streets for money. The blind boy with the fine voice was the biggest earner in Alfie's gang.

How Sammy would envy Richard and how he would love to have a chance to sing in the most famous church in London, Westminster Abbey itself! Alfie thought hard, shushing Richard when he tried to speak.

'We'll manage,' he said eventually. And then after a minute, 'So you just come into the Abbey and go to your places before the service?'

'That's right,' said Richard, 'and it's not fair; the rest of the school are still out enjoying themselves.'

That was good news to hear. That meant that he and Richard would be able to go through the school up to the organist's room without the danger of meeting hordes of boys.

'And the church would be as dark as this?'

'Even darker. Evensong starts at four o'clock and at this time of year the place is as black as pitch, except for the candles, of course.'

'And people, ordinary people, are allowed into the service.'

'That's right.'

Alfie sat back with a grin. He loved this sort of thing. He was a great planner. He worked out the details in his mind.

Sarah, he thought. She was always neatly and tidily dressed in good clothes these days. She could accompany Sammy to the church. Somehow they would get him into the seat ahead of time.

'My friend, East, sits next to me. We could tell him the secret.' Richard was peering at Alfie's face in the dim light.

He was a funny fellow, Alfie decided. Why on earth would he climb the roof of the Abbey at night when all the other boys were tucked up in their beds? He never took another boy with him; he had told Alfie that. He lived on excitement. Alfie had known a few people like that – mostly they went to the bad, and made a living robbing coaches or breaking into houses . . .

Still, it's none of my business, he thought, rising to his feet. 'Let's go,' he said.

First Richard had to listen to Sammy's voice. If that was good enough – and Alfie had no idea of the difference between an alto and a treble – then, in the hours that remained to them before four o'clock, Richard could teach Sammy whatever song was going to be sung that night.

And, while the service of evensong was being

sung and while the organ was being played by Mr Ivanov, then Richard and Alfie could find the evidence to prove that Boris, as Richard called him, was the Russian spy wanted by Scotland Yard.

CHAPTER 10

SAMMY
SINGS

Tom and Mutsy were doing tricks in Trafalgar Square
when Richard and Alfie arrived. Tom held up a card
with a picture of four rats and Mutsy gave four short
barks and then whined.

'Stay, Mutsy,' whispered Alfie as he saw the dog's
head swivel towards him. He knew that, despite the
noise of the horses' hoofs, the cab drivers' shouts or
the street sellers' cries of *'Hot muffins for sale'*, Mutsy,
the genius dog, would hear his master's voice and
obey.

Tom, on the other hand, gave the two well-dressed young gentlemen just a quick glance and went on impressing the small crowd in front of him with Mutsy's knowledge of arithmetic. Alfie giggled to himself as he watched. Obviously Tom had not recognised him.

The pair was doing well. Mutsy barked ten times at the picture of ten rats, and the pennies rained down when he did a little dance on his hind legs, picked up a tin plate from the ground and carried it carefully from person to person, his lips pulled back from his teeth in obedience to Tom's command to smile. From time to time, his brown eyes rested on Alfie with such a look of longing that Alfie found it hard to resist spoiling the act by going and patting him.

'My dog,' he said proudly to Richard when Mutsy had deposited the plate, heavy with coins, at Tom's feet. Alfie snapped his fingers and Mutsy came to him immediately, winding himself round and round Alfie's legs in an ecstasy of love.

'Mutsy!' said Tom, scandalised at the dog's behaviour towards a well-dressed young toff.

'He's not doing any harm,' said Alfie, trying to speak in a toff's voice; but Tom was not deceived. His eyes widened and he glanced quickly around.

'You go ahead,' said Alfie in a low voice. 'We'll be along in a while. Where's Sammy? And Jack?'

'Jack's gone to get some coal out of the river for the fire and Sammy's at home with Sarah. He was a bit worried when you didn't come home. Said he didn't have the heart to sing this morning.' Tom mumbled the words as he started to put the cards back into their box. He did not look at the two well-dressed young gentlemen, but discreetly kept his attention on what he was doing. His sharp eyes had flickered across the square to a heavily built man standing by one of the two fountains and in a minute he and Mutsy were gone.

The man did not look after Tom; his attention was on Richard. Although he was not wearing the fur coat today, but a plain black wool cloak-like garment, Alfie immediately recognised him as the organist from Westminster. He nudged Richard, but it was too late. Boris came plunging across.

'You there, young master! You're one of the boys from the choir at Westminster School, aren't you? Young Master Richard Green; that's right, isn't it?'

Rapidly Alfie slid behind the chestnut seller. There

was little he could do for Richard now – just watch and listen.

'I've been looking at the headmaster's punishment book and I see that you were punished a few months ago because you were seen on the roof of the Abbey at night-time. Were you there last night?'

'No, sir! Certainly not, sir!' Richard sounded quite shocked at the idea.

'Don't you lie to me! I know there were a couple of boys on the roof last night. I saw one go up myself. That one wasn't you; it was a rough boy from the slums, a bare-footed boy; but the policeman said he caught a glimpse of two boys and one of them was wearing a hat. Now you're going to be in trouble, Green, unless you tell me where I can find that other boy, the bare-footed lad.'

Alfie froze, standing very still. What would Richard do? He knew nothing of the Westminster choirboy; he had just shared a few dangerous hours with him. Richard had no responsibility for him. What would he decide? Would he betray Alfie?

'*Boy*, sir?' Richard sounded puzzled. He was certainly a good actor. Alfie could see how his eyes glittered with excitement.

There was a note of uncertainty in the Russian's voice when he said, 'It was you on the roof last night, wasn't it?'

He doesn't know, thought Alfie with relief. He just checked through the punishment book until he found the name of someone who had once climbed the roof of the Abbey.

Richard gave a light laugh. 'Not me, sir. Browne Minor had some goodies, a nice tuck-box of cake and pasties from home in Kent last night, sir. We had a bit of a feast, sir.'

Boris Ivanov stared at him intently while Alfie held his breath. Richard looked relaxed and slightly amused and waited quietly until the organist turned on his heel and strode off.

'He'll have it in for you now,' said Alfie, rejoining him.

Richard shrugged. 'Not worried,' he said. 'He's not important; Mr Ffoulkes is in charge of the choir and he's not going to have me expelled. I told you, I'm the best treble in the choir, and he needs me. Boris is not even a proper master, he's only the organist. Let's go and see your brother.'

* * *

68

'Did you get a chance to see what was written on the paper that he pulled out of the postbox?' Back at the cellar, Sarah was her usual clear-headed, thoughtful self. She had welcomed Richard, glad that she had bullied Jack and Tom into tidying up the cellar to pass the long hours this morning while they had been waiting for news of Alfie. Sammy had been given the task of cleaning the frying pan and kettle, and she herself had washed the one small window that looked onto the pavement. There was a cosy fire because Jack had brought in a new lot of coal which he had picked out from the River Thames at the place where the coal barges moored by Hungerford Bridge.

The cellar looked bright and cheerful, she thought with satisfaction as she looked around. It was lit by firelight and filled with the smell of sausages, bought with one of Inspector Denham's sixpences and now frying gently on the pan placed on top of the glowing coals.

Sarah saw Richard give an admiring glance around, commenting on how cosy it was and seating himself beside the fire. Alfie seemed pleased with his praise, though Sarah reckoned that to a Westminster schoolboy like Richard it was probably a very poor place. He wanted to please, she thought, but quickly turned her attention back to the solving of the spy mystery. The five pounds that Inspector Denham promised would keep the boys safe in the cellar for the rest of the winter. The puzzle had to be solved.

'Just drawings,' Alfie was saying. 'I couldn't see very well.'

'And the paper that he ate?' asked Tom. 'Imagine eating a piece of paper! What was written on that?'

'Sort of nonsense,' said Alfie with a frown. He was proud of his quick brain and hated not to understand things straight away. '*The quick brown fox jumps over the lazy dog*,' he said reluctantly and Tom sniggered. 'I think it had some numbers on it too, but I didn't see them properly. They was written too small,' added Alfie.

'Easy to remember,' said Sarah thoughtfully. 'Look how you remember it, although you only saw it for a second. Must mean something. *The quick brown fox jumps over the lazy dog.*'

'Don't see how,' argued Tom. 'What could foxes and dogs have to do with Russian spies?'

'Perhaps it's just the first part of the message,' said Sammy quietly. It was the first sentence that he had spoken since he heard about the plan for him to sing at Westminster Abbey with the other choirboys. That had brought a flush of excitement to his pale cheeks.

Richard looked across at him. He had been a little embarrassed about how to deal with a blind boy, but now he had got used to it.

'Let's have a go at the *Magnificat*, Sammy,' he said, stuffing the last sausage into his mouth and tipping some more beer into his mug. 'By Jove, I like your tipple! Good for the throat, this sort of stuff. The boys at Westminster School used to always have beer, but now they just have tea. Beer's much better,' he said approvingly.

'I've listened to your choir practising it,' said Sammy confidently. 'I only know the first verse, though. You'll have to teach me the rest.' He stood up unselfconsciously and began to sing. Even Tom was frozen into stillness as Sammy's high, pure voice filled the little cellar and echoed from the rafters overhead.

'My God! You're better than me! You reached that high C more easily than I do. You'd better sing softly or else old Ffoulkes, blind as a bat though he is, will scent out a stranger.' Richard sounded very taken aback and Alfie smiled to himself at the Westminster boy's astonishment. He supposed it did seem amazing that a poor boy like Sammy could sing as well as the best choirboys of Westminster. He felt pleased that his brother had won the approval of a toff like Richard.

'Do all the boys go to evensong, or is it just the choir?' Sarah was working out how they would get a blind boy into the choir stalls of Westminster Abbey without anyone noticing. Pity that Tom was not the musical one, she thought, but then, when she saw Sammy's face, flushed with excitement, she changed her mind. Poor Sammy, he did not have a great life. Singing with the most famous boy choristers in the whole of London would be a wonderful thing for him – something that he would look back on for years.

Life's not fair, thought Sarah, not for the first time. She was not especially musical herself, but it was easy to hear that Sammy had a purer, higher voice than Richard and yet Richard had been in the Westminster choir for four years, with singing lessons twice a day.

Why was it that Sammy had no chance of a life like that?

Why was it that Alfie seemed so keen to impress a boy like Richard? Jack, who was shy and modest, had not said a word and Tom was showing off a bit too much. Why, she asked herself, was *she* so pleased that she had tidied up the cellar before Richard's visit? He was just a boy of their own age. Did having money and going to a swell's school make you more important?

And why was it that Alfie, with all his brains, had to risk his life to earn a few pounds to keep the four boys housed and fed?

CHAPTER 11

PERIL
AT THE ABBEY

By the time the church bells sounded three in the afternoon, Alfie had dressed Sammy in the clothes that Richard had lent; the clothes belonging to Smith Minor, the boy with measles. He, himself, was glad to put his own ragged clothes on again. Tom had sneered at his 'toff's rig-out' and they had quarrelled and Tom had flung out of the cellar in a fit of temper. Jack had disappeared soon after. Alfie was pleased neither was there when it came to changing back.

If it came to a chase he would prefer bare feet and

knee-length breeches, he thought as he brushed the shoulders of the black frock coat and placed the top hat on Sammy's newly washed blond curls.

'Sammy and Richard look quite alike,' said Sarah as she came back from the shop with a pair of thick socks. She looked critically at the blind boy and nodded. They were the same height and had the same blond curly hair. 'Try the boots with those socks, now, Sammy,' she suggested.

And that worked well. The thick pair of socks meant that the boots fitted his feet. Richard straightened the hat, adjusting the elastic to fit Sammy's head.

'Take off your hat when you get inside the Abbey,' he ordered. 'And then when you get to the place in the choir you'll have to put on your surplice – just pull it over your head. I can't do that for you.' Richard sounded nervous.

'Don't fuss,' snapped Sarah, who was feeling anxious herself. 'We've got it all set up. If the Abbey is as dark as you say, then Tom can easily make his way under the seats and be behind the choir stalls before you walk over with Sammy. He'll help him if necessary. When the service is over, you just change places. I'll take Sammy out and you go back into school with your friends.'

'And I'll be in that passageway behind the choir stalls,' said Jack.

'Don't forget to sing softly, Sammy,' said Richard for the tenth time. 'You don't want to make old Ffoulkes suspicious.'

'What are you worrying about? It's easier than jumping across a four-foot space when you're thirty feet above the ground,' said Alfie with a grin and was pleased when Richard grinned back.

Me, Alfie, friends with a toff, he thought with wonderment. And such a toff, too! He was still amazed whenever he thought of that scene where Richard jumped the gap without hesitating. There was no doubt that Richard was full of courage – a bit foolhardy, even. Strange that he was so anxious about Sammy taking his place. There must be something about this Mr Ffoulkes that made him nervous, decided Alfie. He was glad that his new friend had not shown these signs of nervousness in front of Tom. Tom would have been bound to sneer at him.

'You can walk into the choir stalls with Sammy,

Richard, and then you can be sure that he is in the right place,' ordered Sarah. 'Keep your head; don't take any risks. No point in showing off.' She sounded severe, and a little worried, so Alfie hastened to reassure her.

'Richard says that it's so dark that the choirboys have to feel their way,' he said and then he turned to Richard. 'What about me? Where do I go? Where do I wait for you?' He could hardly wait to get into the rooms of Boris the Russian organist and spy. What was in that brown-paper wrapped parcel? Even as he listened to Richard's instructions, he was wondering about that parcel.

And then there was that strange sentence: *The quick brown fox jumps over the lazy dog*. Alfie repeated it over to himself again and again, frightened of forgetting it. It must be of huge importance for a man to eat the paper that it was written on.

The Dark Cloister was very damp and smelled of old, dead things. It had stone pillars set at intervals all the way along it and the ceiling was so low that it was only just above Alfie's head. It was very dark, also, and once Alfie had gone a few yards from the entrance he had to grope his way like a blind man, moving from pillar to pillar. After that he stayed still and waited. It seemed a very long time until the pounding of feet on the stone slabs told Alfie that Richard was coming.

'Don't know how you run in the pitch dark like that,' he grunted as Richard came to a stop beside him.

'We always do that, Smith Minor and myself. You just get into the middle of the Dark Cloister and then start to run. Some fellows' nerve fails them – the ghosts of the old monks from eight hundred years ago are supposed to haunt the Dark Cloister,' said Richard. Then he added airily, 'I say, do you believe in ghosts? You can hear them chanting the old Latin chants sometimes. I've heard them myself, in this very place. It's the oldest building in the place and there's a cellar beneath it where no one dares to go.'

Boys' stuff, thought Alfie, not bothering to answer. He had no interest in ghosts and no idea what happened eight hundred years ago. Survival was what was important and in order to survive in

London these days you needed three things: food, shelter and fire – in that order. These schoolboys had never had to trouble themselves about having to get these essentials for life, so they frightened themselves with ghosts.

'Let's get on with it,' he said. 'Get that key to the organist's door.'

As soon as I see what's in that parcel, I'll go straight to Inspector Denham and tell him the whole story, Alfie decided. It was obvious how information was passed to the Russian Embassy and why Inspector Denham or the men from Scotland Yard had not been able to lay their hands on the guilty Member of Parliament, whether it was Ron Shufflebottom from Yorkshire, Tom Craddock from Cornwall, or Roland Valentine from Essex. Whichever of these was the spy, they were using Boris Ivanov, the Russian organist at Westminster to make contact with the Russian Embassy.

'All the spare keys hang in a little room outside the headmaster's study. He won't have locked it before going across to the Abbey. The servants need the keys to bring in the fresh coal and make up the fires for the evening.'

Richard sounded very carefree and led the way into the school, walking confidently along the dimly lit passageways. Alfie followed cautiously, stepping from one pool of shadows into another and keeping well back when Richard cautiously turned the handle to a door.

Even Alfie was taken aback when it was suddenly thrown open and a furious voice said, 'Boy, what are you doing here?'

'Sorry, sir! Sorry to disturb you, sir! Mr Ffoulkes wanted to know if you were coming to the service, sir.' Alfie had to admire Richard's ready imagination. But would it work? He held his breath.

'I've told him already that I have a headache.' The headmaster sounded more irritated than annoyed. Alfie drew in a breath of relief, but too soon.

'Who's that boy there? Someone's over there. I heard someone. Who is it?'

Quickly Alfie grabbed a top hat from a shelf in the dark passageway and placed it on his head. The headmaster held up his candle and peered through the gloom. Out of the corner of his eye, Alfie saw a shadow of a boy in a top hat on the wall behind him. There was nothing he could do about his bare legs and his torn clothes, but in the dim light he might pass for a Westminster scholar.

'That's Wilkins, sir. He's not well; Mr Ffoulkes told me to take him back to the dormitory, sir.'

'Very well. Now leave me in peace!' The headmaster slammed the outer door shut and Alfie heard a key turn in the lock.

'That's torn it,' whispered Richard returning to Alfie. 'He usually never bothers locking that outside door. Now what will we do? Should we get out on the roof and then climb in through his window? It's probably locked, of course. We'll have to smash the glass.'

He sounded quite unconcerned about smashing the glass in the organist's room and once again Alfie thought how reckless his new friend was. Perhaps if he, Alfie, had always had money and people calling him *sir*, he would have been as reckless as Richard. As it was, he could see problems in smashing windows. There must be another way.

Alfie thought for a moment and then smiled to himself. It was worth a try.

'Let's go up to your study,' he murmured in Richard's ear, but said no more until they were safely inside the little room with the door closed behind them. Only then did he open the cupboard and remove the board and show Richard how he had climbed up the wall to the attic.

'I know what it was,' said Richard, holding the candle up high and peering up into the dim, cobwebby space between the wooden panelling and the stone wall. 'Westminster School was the old monks' place in the past, and it was so cold and damp that they built a wooden wall inside the stone to make little rooms. Some master told me that. I say, do you bet all the rooms are like this? I'd say they probably are. Do you think that we can get into any of the rooms in the same way?'

'It's easy to climb up,' said Alfie. 'But can we get down into the organist's room? That's the question?'

'Should do,' said Richard confidently. 'It's on the other side of the building; but it's on the top floor so it should be easy to get down to it, if the other side is the same as this.'

They climbed the stone wall, Alfie leading the way, finding footholds on the wooden beams. Despite Richard's confidence, they went into quite a few wrong rooms until they eventually arrived at Boris the organist's room. By this time the two boys were covered with cobwebs and streaked with dust and dirt. Richard gave a worried look at the clock on the mantelpiece.

'Just twenty minutes to go,' he grunted as he lit a candle from the embers of the fire. 'I say, if we find something perhaps we should try blackmailing him. We'll just get a pat on the back if we hand him over to the police.'

'I've been promised five pounds,' said Alfie. He wondered whether he should share it with Richard and was relieved when the Westminster boy laughed.

'Five pounds?' he said. 'That's just a fleabite! My father would give me five pounds just to get me out of his sight. We'd get more than that from Boris.'

Alfie did not answer. For him, five pounds was a fortune, but he didn't want to admit this. Quickly he looked around the room. The table was covered with grubby piles of notebooks and many loose sheets of paper. There was a tray with inkpots filled with black, green and red ink and a pile of neatly trimmed feather pens.

But there was no small, brown-paper wrapped parcel.

Where would the owner of the room put something important, wondered Alfie. He searched the cupboard, but only clothes and a musty old gown hung there. A quick hunt through the top shelf only turned up a mortarboard and a few tattered books of music.

Richard crawled under the bed, but came out with empty hands.

Then Alfie had an inspiration. He went to the bookcase and pulled out the books in clusters of five or six at a time. There was nothing on the top shelf, but then, on the second shelf, he struck lucky. There was something behind a set of dictionaries.

'Come on,' groaned Richard. 'We've got to get back to the Abbey. If Sammy is discovered I'll be flayed alive.'

'Here it is,' said Alfie. He pulled out the wrapped parcel. It had been opened and then re-wrapped; he could see that. The red wax seal had been broken. Quickly he took the box to the table, undid the knot on the string and spread out the paper, waiting eagerly to see what was inside it.

It was a box of sweets!

Alfie pulled up the lid and smelled them. 'Real sweets,' he said, baffled.

'Let's have one each,' said Richard with a grin, though he still looked nervous. He recited some of the names of sweets that he recognised aloud: chocolate, truffle, Turkish Delight, fudge.

'Better not,' said Alfie. 'Might be poisoned.' He spoke absent-mindedly, because a slip of paper had fallen from the lid of the box of sweets. Picking it up, he saw it had a series of numbers on it.

'Write these numbers quick,' he said to Richard and, with one more worried look at the clock, Richard copied the figures onto a scrap of paper, using black ink and shaking some sand over the paper when he had finished. Alfie shoved the paper into his pocket, giving a hasty glance at the clock on the mantelpiece. Only fifteen minutes to go!

'We'd better not take them – too risky,' he said, making sure that the slip was placed back in the same position inside the lid and then folding the brown paper over the sweet box. He was just about to tie the twine when he saw Richard's eyes widen with horror.

There had been a click from the lock.

And a sound of the door handle turning.

And the heavy velvet curtain hanging in front of

the door moved in the draught.

'The headmaster!' whispered Richard.

Alfie froze. There was no time to escape.

And then suddenly . . .

'Headmaster!' called a voice from the corridor outside.

CHAPTER 12

RISKS

'Who's in there?' said an irritable voice. And then, 'Yes, yes, Mr Irwin. I'll attend to that in a moment. I just want to find a book that I lent to Mr Ivanov.'

'It is the headmaster!' Richard looked around wildly. White-faced, he blew out the candle. 'Let's get up to the attic,' he whispered.

'No, we'll be trapped there. Let's get out of here.' Instantly Alfie acted. *Might as well take these things now – the headmaster will tell Boris that someone was in his room*, he said to himself. He shoved the

87

box of sweets into his pocket and went over to the window, feeling his way in the darkness. He fumbled for the handle and pushed it open. A damp draught of foggy air streamed into their faces. Alfie climbed out onto the slates.

'You go first,' he said. 'Get straight up onto the roof. I'll count up to six to give you a start. I'll let him have a sight of me so that he doesn't suspect you.'

Then they had some bad luck. Just below them in Dean's Yard was a gas lamp and, as Richard climbed onto the windowsill, it was lit with a *pop*. The lamplighter moved on back out through the gate without looking upwards, but now the two would be visible. However, there was little that the headmaster could do to a ragged boy climbing out of the window, reckoned Alfie. He would make a great fuss. He would shout, yell and send for the police; but by that time he and Richard would be on the roof of the Abbey and could climb down on the far side.

The roar of *Stop, thief!* came almost immediately. Alfie glanced back and saw a red-faced man wearing a mortarboard leaning out of the widely-opened window. Luckily he was looking down, not up. Alfie did not wait any longer. Richard was probably on the Abbey roof by now. Quickly he dragged himself up, holding onto the stone ledge at the end of the roof.

In a moment he was on the roof ridge. There was no response to the headmaster's cries and Alfie guessed that most of the servants took their rest during the service at the Abbey. In any case, the organ was now playing very loudly and the booming notes filled the little yard with noise.

Alfie stayed where he was for the moment. A few seconds later, he saw the silhouette of a black hat against the night sky. Richard was over at the north side of the Abbey. There was a small door there. If Richard could get down quickly, he would still be in time to swap places with Sammy in the choir stalls.

Then the sound of singing came to him. Someone must have opened the west door. Soon the people would be coming out.

'*My soul doth magnify the Lord,*' sang the high, sweet voices of the choir, and Alfie almost thought that he could distinguish Sammy's voice from amongst them. He listened intently. There was no sign of Richard now, so hopefully he would have got down before this hymn had finished.

Then the organ began to play again and the voices of all the churchgoers, deep and high, mingled in the words.

Alfie had often heard Sammy sing this and he mouthed the words to himself as he jumped the gap and landed on the roof of Westminster Abbey.

'*Glory to thee, my God, this night,*' sang the congregation as Alfie edged his way across the roof of the south cloister.

'*For all the blessings of the light,*' he hummed tunelessly as he made his way past the devil's head.

'*Keep me, O keep me, King of Kings,*
Beneath thy own almighty wings.'

Now the sung words were getting fainter as he reached the centre of the Abbey roof.

Everything seemed easier this time and soon he was over on the north side of the Abbey, listening to the organ thunder out the last few notes and then suddenly fall silent.

Did that mean that the service was finished, wondered Alfie. And if so, had Richard had time to change places with Sammy before the choir had to file their way out of the church, and back down the Dark Cloister? Each boy would be holding a lighted candle, so it was important that the swap was made before the procession took place.

Alfie stood up beside a statue and peered down. The people were beginning to stream out of the Abbey. Some were talking and others were just looking for cabs. There was no air of excitement about them, though. No sign of anything unusual happening.

And then he saw a pair of figures that he recognised. One was a girl in a thick, respectable-looking black cloak and the other was a blond boy wearing a suit and carrying a top hat. The two were linked together, the girl's arm tucked into the boy's arm. Alfie smiled as he looked. Sarah would walk with Sammy as far as Trafalgar Square and then she would hand him over to Tom and Jack while she went off to her evening's work at the White Horse Inn. They would have to get Smith Minor's suit and top hat back to Richard but in the meantime, thought Alfie proudly, Sammy looked a treat in it.

As for me, thought Alfie, I'm better off staying where I am for the moment. There seemed to be a lot of policemen around the Abbey tonight and he would stay for an hour or two on the roof to give everything time to calm down.

CHAPTER 13

TROUBLE

'Richard was great, wasn't he?' Alfie burst in through the door of the cellar, giving Mutsy a quick pat on the head. They were all there. Sammy, though still looking unusually clean and tidy, had changed out of the smart clothes and was wearing his own ragged breeches and torn coat. He turned his head eagerly when Alfie came in, but turned back to the fire again when he heard his brother's words.

'*Richard, Richard, Richard,*' sneered Tom. 'What's so great about Richard? Just a toffy-nosed, flash-talking swell. Who cares about him? We're sick of him, aren't we, Jack?'

Jack said nothing, just looked troubled.

'I suppose you don't need me tonight, then,' said Tom. 'Is your precious Richard going to hang around street corners getting freezing cold? I can just see him! You know what he's going to do, don't you, just as soon as he gets tired of you? He'll play the informer, and then you'll find yourself in hot water. If ever I saw a snitch, well, he's one.'

'You shut your mouth and get out of here,' said Alfie hotly.

'C'mon, Tom, I need a hand,' said Jack, the peacemaker. He steered Tom quickly past Alfie and they could be heard arguing on the cellar steps.

'He's just jealous,' said Sarah, as the voices disappeared. 'He likes working with you.'

Alfie said nothing. He frowned at the fire while Sarah told him all about how well Sammy had done and how a lady beside her in the Abbey had whispered to her that she had never heard the choir sing so beautifully as they sang that night.

Then Alfie recounted how he and Richard had stolen the box of sweets from the organist's room. 'Do you know what I'm going to do now?' he continued when neither Sarah nor Sammy responded. 'I've just decided, I'm going to wrap up a parcel that looks just like that and tie it to a key in just the same way as they did before and I'm going to put it into the postbox and see what happens.' He looked at Sarah. 'What do you think? Will it work?'

'What do you hope will happen?' asked Sarah, narrowing her eyes.

Alfie clicked his tongue in an annoyed fashion. If he had said that to Richard there would have been an immediate response of 'What a lark!'

'One of them men, one of them MPs, will pull it out, of course, and then I'll know the truth,' he said impatiently.

'And what will happen if none of them goes near to the postbox, if none of them touches it?'

'Oh, pipe down, Sarah.' Alfie could feel himself exploding with exasperation.

'I think,' said Sarah, 'that you should go straight to Inspector Denham. Tell him everything and let him sort it out. This business is dangerous. Sammy took quite a risk today for you.' Her voice rose and shook slightly. 'If he had been discovered, they might have put him in the workhouse. I was worried sick! I say that you should stop now – stop all this nonsense, climbing around roofs at night and breaking into schools. Go to Inspector Denham.'

'I didn't mind,' said Sammy firmly.

Somehow these few words from Sammy made Alfie feel worse than ever. However, he was determined to solve the problem and earn the promised reward of five pounds. He turned an annoyed gaze towards Sarah.

'Well I'm not going to Inspector Denham yet,' he said hotly. He went to the cupboard, took out an old rusty key, carefully re-wrapped the brown paper parcel with some twine belonging to his father, who had been a cobbler, and stuck some cobbler's wax to fasten the twine and its dangling key securely to the paper. When that was done he gave a brief look around and said, 'I'm off. Stay, Mutsy!'

Westminster Abbey was quiet and dark, with only a few pinpricks of light showing through the stained-glass windows when Alfie arrived outside it. He walked around for a while before approaching the red pillar box with *Victoria Regina* in gold letters just below its slot. He gave one more glance around before dropping the small parcel, attached to the key, into it.

Then he strolled for a while around the Abbey until he found a shadowy corner and began to climb up to the roof.

It was funny, he thought, how much work the men who built the Abbey, all those hundreds of years ago, had put it into it. Not content with just building walls and roofs, they had decorated almost every inch with little twists and curls, stone heads, carved patterns, statues of saints and angels. *Must have had a lot of time on their hands to give themselves all that work*, he said to himself as he grabbed a head and inserted his toes into a stone flower. Still he was grateful to them. It made the roof a joy to climb.

He looked up and down the long line of Westminster Abbey. He had walked around its pavements often enough, during all the hours that he had spent hanging around waiting for something to happen. The Abbey was about six hundred feet long, he reckoned. Where he stood now was about halfway between the little chapel at one end, and the Great West Door at the other.

The roof over the little chapel was the place to be,

thought Alfie. From there, he could look down over the Houses of Parliament and watch its members come out after a late night sitting.

Tonight would be the night! He felt confident about that. Now he knew how everything worked, he would keep a sharp eye on that postbox and with luck he would soon find out which of the three men was the spy. He would be able to give his name and the name of Boris Ivanov to Inspector Denham.

Inch by inch, Alfie made his way across the roof. There was a low parapet, high enough to hide a six-year-old child, but for a twelve-year-old like Alfie the only possibility was to crawl or to crouch. The razor-sharp edges of the slates cut into his bare knees, but it was better than the agony of walking bent double.

The climb down was long and difficult and, when he was halfway down, the bells sounded and almost deafened him. And then Big Ben started chiming. The new belltower, Big Ben, was a great service to Londoners without watches, thought Alfie. Everyone could keep track of time now as its sound echoed all over the town. He looked across at the great clock face: eight o'clock. He hoped desperately that the MPs would finish whatever they were doing soon. He was cold and stiff, and yawns kept almost dislocating his jaw.

At last he reached the roof of the chapel. This little chapel was no higher than an ordinary London house, and he was now only about twenty feet above ground level. In some ways he was glad to come down as the immense height of the Abbey had begun to make him feel dizzy.

To his dismay the whole roof of the chapel had been covered with sheets of lead – soaking wet from the fog – and it was as slippery as ice. Once again Alfie had to go along on the inside of the parapet, but this was even more difficult as this parapet was lower still and the danger of being seen was much greater.

However, it looked as though his wait would not be a long one. The MPs were streaming out, and there was a queue of cabs lined up, ready to take them to their town houses or to the coaching inns. In ones, or twos or threes they went off, chattering happily.

Some of the last to come out were the three men on the rifle development committee. And there they were, just like before, the three MPs, standing under the gas lamp outside the Houses of Parliament. Alfie could see them quite clearly: two big men and one thin one. Although the air was still foggy, there were no clouds in the sky and, like the night before, a brilliant full moon lit up the whole scene.

But there was a difference. No Russian lurked in the shadows of St Stephen's Tavern; Alfie was sure of that. Boris was probably on his way, even now, to the Russian Embassy. Alfie bit his lip at the thought of the Russians coming to hunt for him, but stayed very still. He might be in danger, but he was determined to see this matter through.

Yes! One of the men, Ron Shufflebottom from Yorkshire, was standing very close to the red pillar box. Unfortunately Roland Valentine was quite near to him, telling jokes as usual. Tom Craddock was at the edge of the pavement whistling for a cab.

And then Ron Shufflebottom lifted a hand and pointed towards the gate into the Houses of Parliament. Roland Valentine turned his head in that direction. Immediately his companion turned back to the postbox and Alfie saw him seize the key and draw up the parcel from its depths. By the time Roland Valentine looked back, the parcel, its thread and its key were safely tucked into Ron Shufflebottom's pocket and they had all piled into a cab together.

The man from Yorkshire was the guilty one.

Now Alfie knew almost the whole story.

Now he could go to Inspector Denham and tell him what happened.

But not yet, he said to himself . . .

Only when the place was empty did Alfie slide down from the roof of the chapel and, after a quick glance to make sure that no one was around, he crossed the road and carefully examined the pillar box.

But there was nothing there: no string tied to a key, no sign of anything left. And there was no sign of Boris Ivanov, the organist and spy.

Alfie thought: even if the organist had gone to the Russian Embassy, Ron Shufflebottom would not know that yet. It would be sensible to go home now, but Alfie had lots of courage.

And lots of curiosity.

Where was Boris? Alfie was determined that when he went to Inspector Denham in the morning he would have the whole story for him.

He made up his mind to go back into the school and to see Richard. With one last look around, he slipped across the road and made his way around the

Abbey. He kept well into the shadow of that huge building until he reached the spot where he had climbed up last night when he had been rescued by Richard.

It was funny how much easier it all seemed to him now. His feet instinctively found the foot of the stone saint; his hands easily grasped the short length of rope hung there by Richard. The moon was not quite as full as last night's, but there was still enough light for him to make his way in between carved towers and ugly gargoyles and along parapets. When he reached the gap he jumped it almost without thinking. His mind was deeply engaged with the puzzle of why Boris Ivanov had not turned up to send or receive a message from the pillar box from his contact at the Houses of Parliament.

Alfie slid silently along the roof ridge of the school, stopped in the shelter of a warm chimney to catch his breath, and then continued on. Most of the windows were dark, but there was a candle burning in one – that must be the room belonging to the organist.

Cautiously Alfie peered down.

The small square yard at the centre of Westminster School was paved in white stone and the moonlight filled it, illuminating the dark figure lying, face down, arms outstretched, in the middle of it. On the back of the head was a mass of clotted blood and beside the body lay a blood-soaked pole.

Alfie did not hesitate. Grasping a pipe leading down from the gutter, he slid to the ground and approached the still figure.

It was Boris Ivanov.

And he was dead.

CHAPTER 14

THE BLOOD-STAINED CUDGEL

Alfie bent down and picked up the cudgel. It was large and heavy, rounded and smooth at one end and jaggedly broken at the other. Boris Ivanov's skull had been broken by a blow from about the centre of it; that was where the mess of blood and brains had smeared the wood.

A tall man, and a powerful one, must have done this, Alfie thought. And a picture of Ron Shufflebottom, the MP from Yorkshire, came into his head. He was a big man, with wide shoulders and long arms. He could have swung the cudgel with enough power to have broken the man's skull. Would he have been tall enough? Boris was quite tall, but it would perhaps have been easy enough to get him to bend down, to pretend that something had been dropped, perhaps.

But when was Boris Ivanov killed? Could Ron Shufflebottom have got out from the Houses of Parliament, done the murder and then rejoined his friends?

Alfie picked up the cudgel and gave it an experimental swing, holding it firmly in both hands.

And as he did so, there was a sudden scream.

'Murder! Murder! Catch 'im!'

'In the yard!' screamed another voice. 'Look at 'im. 'e's murdered the organ master!'

A candle appeared in one window to the left, then one to the right and three in front of him. There was the squeak of bolts being drawn open on doors and yells of 'Murder! Murder!' came from every direction. Alfie's head snapped from one direction to the next, like a dog who is being attacked from all sides. He gripped the cudgel with some idea of fighting his way out of the yard. His foot skidded on a piece of wet cardboard on the ground and he almost stumbled, but then recovered himself.

Quickly Alfie ran in the opposite direction towards the stone archway that led out into Dean's Yard. If he could just get out of this place he might be able to outrun them all. But the archway was blocked by a stout wooden door which fitted the archway so well that nothing bigger than a mouse could squeeze through the space beneath it.

There was a large heavy iron bolt across it. Alfie tugged at it frantically, but it was no good. Through a loop in the bolt a massive padlock was fixed and locked securely.

In desperation, Alfie lifted the heavy pole and, using two hands, aimed it at the padlock. At the first jolt the padlock jumped.

'Come on, Bart!' screamed a voice. 'The murderer is escaping while you pull on your britches.'

If only it were true. Alfie breathed a silent prayer that Bart's britches were new and very, very stiff.

'Murder! Murder! Murder!' The shrill cries split the quiet night air.

Bang! For the second time Alfie hit the padlock. For the second time it jumped, but still it remained securely locked.

'Here's a gun, Bart! Shoot 'im, shoot 'im through the window.'

A bullet rang out and bounced against the window of the gatehouse. More screams ran out – this time they had an excited note in them. Broken glass rained down.

'Mind what you're doin', Bart Hegarty,' roared a voice from above Alfie's head. 'You nearly shot me dead, you daft old man.'

'I'm comin', I'm comin'; give a man a chance to make 'imself decent,' replied another voice, presumably Bart's.

Once again Alfie aimed his stout stick at the padlock, but this was a feeble effort. His shoulder was on fire with the jarring of the previous blows. Frantically he looked around. Was there anywhere that he could hide? He spotted a manhole, but it was gleaming in the full light of the moon. That was no good. And who knows where it leads? thought Alfie. No, there was only one chance for him now.

Alfie dropped the stick – it was no protection against a gun. He moved out of the moonlight and into the shadows beside the first house on the left-hand side of the yard. Grasping the downpipe, he began to lever himself upwards. The flagpole had been broken off. So was that where the heavy cudgel had come from?

'Where's 'e gone?'

Then there was an exuberant yell from the top-floor dormitory where the boys slept.

'Tally-ho!' roared thirty voices.

'The fox has gone to ground!'

'Hunt him out!'

'Yay-hoo!'

The excited sounds echoed through the little yard. All the boys were awake and cheering on the hunt from the dormitory windows.

A shot was fired towards the wooden gate. Alfie heard it splinter the wood and there were more shouts. He shut them out of his head and concentrated hard, trying to control his breathing so that they would not hear him pant. Spread-eagled against the side of the house like this, he would make an easy target.

Luckily the boys continued to scream and shout. They probably went fox hunting when they were at home in the country, thought Alfie. He remembered stories his grandfather used to tell him of how the rich people mounted their horses and took their dogs to chase one poor little fox. Alfie sent a quick prayer for help up to the heaven where he supposed his grandfather now lived and concentrated on pulling himself up, slowly, hand over hand, by Richard's rope towards the roof.

Now he could believe that his prayers were answered. There was a window open a few feet above him. And the wonderful thing was that there was no hint of candlelight from it. It would probably be one of those rooms for the boys, Alfie guessed. What was it Richard had called them? *Studies.* Yes, that would be it: the study of a careless boy who had left the window open before he had gone to bed. If he could only get in there, he would be able to make his way behind the wooden panelling and up to the attic. He could hide there until the hunt was given up and then make his way across the school roof and over onto the Abbey before dawn arrived.

Another few feet, Alfie told himself and then his eyes widened at the sight of a splotch of yellow light on the wall only a few feet away from him. He risked a glance over his shoulder. Yes, someone had the brains to bring out a lantern, and he was using it to scan every inch of the wall.

Alfie made one last superhuman effort, levered himself up the last few feet, edged his knee onto the windowsill and shot, head first, into the room.

'Got you!' said a voice.

CHAPTER 15

CAPTURED

Alfie wriggled desperately but received a blow from a clenched fist that made his head ring. Dizzy and sick with the impact, he froze. This was often the best thing to do; he knew that from experience. His attacker might relax if he felt that Alfie was cowed. And in the meantime his head might stop spinning.

It was no good, though. A hand crept around his neck, squeezing hard. Alfie coughed and almost lost consciousness. His attacker relaxed the pressure slightly and lit a candle from the embers of the fire.

'Now let's have a look at you,' said a voice and Alfie found himself face to face with the choirmaster, Mr Ffoulkes, the man that Richard so feared.

He had climbed into Mr Ffoulkes' study and was now helpless in his hands.

'I've got him! I've got the murderer!' the choirmaster shouted out of the window and there was a great cheering from the dormitory above.

'Good old Ffoulkes!' shouted one.

'Three cheers for Mr Ffoulkes!' yelled another.

The man just smiled dourly. Still squeezing Alfie's throat with one hand, he reached across and slipped the cord from his dressing gown. In a moment, Alfie found that his hands were knotted behind his back with the cord. It bit into the skin of his wrists and there was little that he could do to free himself. So he did not try; he just waited grimly to see what would happen next.

'Bart,' shouted Mr Ffoulkes. 'Get the headmaster, will you? I'll keep the murderer here until he comes. It's for him to decide what to do with him.'

Alfie waited. He would say nothing until he was in the hands of the police. Then, in the morning, he could ask for Inspector Denham to be sent for. He could tell of Alfie's mission to discover the Russian spy. He would be able to speak up for Alfie.

Or would he?

Could he?

Westminster was under the rule of the police at Scotland Yard. They were more important than the police at Bow Street.

Alfie felt the sharp edge of the cord bite into his wrists and thought of all that was against him.

Not only was he found just beside the dead man's body, but he was actually seen with the blood-stained weapon in his hand.

Perhaps, despite all that Inspector Denham could say, he would be accused of the murder of Boris Ivanov and would be dragged off to Newgate Prison and kept there to await his trial. He had been in Newgate once before and had no wish to set foot in there ever again.

'He's just a boy!' The headmaster burst through the door, followed by an elderly man.

'That's the fellow, sir,' cried the old man. 'That's the fellow! I swear my life to it, sir. I aimed my gun at him, sir. Only just missed, sir.'

'Quiet, Bart!' exclaimed the headmaster. He looked

closely at Alfie. He's very thin,' he said, half to himself. And then, solemnly, to Alfie, 'Did you kill our organist, boy? Now tell the truth, boy, it will be better for your immortal soul. God hates a liar, you know.'

He must think that I'm stupid, thought Alfie. Imagine getting yourself hanged if you could escape by telling a lie! Aloud, he said, 'No, sir, I never. I wouldn't do a thing like that, sir.' He gulped a little, wondering how to account for his presence in the yard.

'I was on top of the roof of Westminster Abbey, sir, listening to the sacred music and looking up at the moon in the heavens, sir,' he said, making his voice sound as sincere as he could. By now there was a huge audience of boys, including Richard, all standing around outside the door in the corridor or else on the stairs. Every one of them was staring at him.

'And then, and then . . .' he went on, dragging out the words while he tried to think. Now came the difficult bit. How could he account for his presence in the little yard?

'And then I saw a man lying on the paving stones. I thought he might have had a fit, sir, so I climbed down to him and then . . .' Alfie gave another gulp and hung his head, trying to look innocent and truthful, and not like the sort of boy that would commit murder.

'You can't believe this nonsense, Headmaster,' said the choirmaster with a sneer.

'I fired my gun at him,' said old Bart with pride.

'He sounds like an honest boy,' said the headmaster hesitantly.

Sounds hoarse, anyway, thought Alfie, working a little saliva into his mouth and allowing it to slide down his sore throat. That choirmaster had nearly strangled him, he thought indignantly.

'Why don't you send Bart down to Scotland Yard for the police,' said Mr Ffoulkes impatiently.

'Perhaps that would be best.' The headmaster didn't sound too happy and Alfie tried to give him an appealing look.

'I'm not goin' out in them streets at this hour of the night,' said Bart. 'All the scum will be out, robbing and murdering.'

'Don't be ridiculous,' said the choirmaster.

'I've worked for this school, man and boy, for nigh on sixty-five years and now you send me out in the middle of the night to a certain death,' said Bart pathetically.

The choirmaster made a contemptuous noise between his lips, but he did not offer to go himself, noticed Alfie. Bart was right, of course; the streets around Westminster were dangerous at this time of night.

'He's correct, you know.' The headmaster sounded more cheerful. 'Let's keep the boy until the morning. I'll talk to him then by daylight. I pride myself on knowing whether a boy is telling the truth or not. I can read it in his face.'

'Leave him here, then, in my room, and give me your gun, Bart,' said Mr Ffoulkes grimly.

Alfie shivered. He would be dead by morning, he thought. *Shot while trying to escape.* That would be the story that Mr Ffoulkes would tell, he reckoned. He shivered again and looked appealingly at the headmaster.

Suddenly Mr Ffoulkes whirled around and stared across at Richard. 'You boy, you, Green, have I seen you with this boy?'

'No, sir,' said Richard in an assured fashion. 'No way, sir! Catch me associating with a fellow like that. Think of the fleas! Never saw him in my life before, sir.'

The choirmaster grunted but he said no more, just gave Alfie another shake and held out a hand towards the gun.

'What about shutting him in the cellar under the Dark Cloister, Headmaster?' suggested Bart. 'He won't get out of that in a hurry. It's got a lock on it the size of a footstool.'

'Yes, let's do that.' The headmaster looked happier. 'And, Bart, Mr Ivanov . . .'

'Don't you worry about that, sir,' said Bart. 'I'll drag 'im into one of the sheds so that it don't upset the young gentlemen in the morning. And that cudgel wot killed him! That's evidence, that is. All over with blood, it is.'

'I'll put the boy in the cellar while you're dealing with the body, Bart. Come on, you!'

Mr Ffoulkes clutched Alfie around the throat – it seemed to be his favourite method – and began to drag him out of the door.

'I'll take the key, Headmaster,' he called over his shoulder. 'I'll make sure that this young man is safely locked up.'

CHAPTER 16

TRAPPED IN THE CELLAR

Alfie's nerves were on edge as the choirmaster dragged him by the throat down the stairs and along the Dark Cloister. No wonder Richard was so scared of this fellow. All the boys were; he sensed that.

Alfie could feel the waves of hate coming from the man and began to wonder about Mr Ffoulkes. Was he perhaps more than a casual friend to the organist? Was there a possibility that he, too, was in the pay of the Russian Embassy? Would he revenge himself on Alfie for the death of his fellow spy?

Or was he the person who had broken off the flagpole and cracked the skull of Boris Ivanov?

If that was true, then he must be pleased to have a scapegoat in the form of a ragged boy from the slums – a boy that no one would miss, that no one would make a fuss about.

Once they were in the Dark Cloister, Mr Ffoulkes paused by a small lantern on a ledge and thrust his face up close to Alfie's.

'Who are you?' he hissed. When Alfie did not answer, he continued, 'What's your name? Where do you live?' And then, 'What do you know about Mr Ivanov?'

One by one the questions came thudding at him, backed up by blows and kicks, but Alfie said nothing. Sooner or later the man would get tired of this and leave him.

Alfie's mind was working hard as he was finally thrust through a heavy wooden door and the lock clicked outside. The place was freezing cold and stank – almost as though a dead body had been left to rot in a corner. Alfie edged away from the smell and turned his head from side to side. He could see nothing. The cellar seemed to be almost pitch black, but he heard the scampering of feet and knew that the place was infested with rats. He shuddered. Of all things he hated rats. He hoped that they would feast on whatever was rotting and would leave him alone.

He passed his hand over the door, but knew that there was no hope of breaking out. The door was immensely solid. Alfie felt close to despair; but he was tough and would not give into these feelings. With a great effort, he switched off his mind from his present danger and began to think about the body in the courtyard.

Who did kill Boris?

There were a few possibilities.

It could have been someone from the Russian Embassy. Boris may have got greedy and demanded more money. Perhaps he threatened to betray Ron Shufflebottom and a man was sent to dispose of him.

Or was it Ron Shufflebottom who had killed Boris? It was only a stone's throw from the Houses of Parliament to Westminster School. Ron Shufflebottom could have accompanied Boris back through the gate leading into the yard, perhaps promising to give him some more money or to sign a document . . . and, what then?

Or did the bad-tempered choirmaster, Mr Ffoulkes, have anything to do with the death of the organist?

The only thing that Alfie felt sure of was that this murder was not planned. Someone planning murder would have brought a weapon. A knife was quick, quiet and very sure. Breaking off a cudgel from a flagpole and then hitting a man over the head was an awkward, risky business. It must have been a sudden impulse, a sudden quarrel, perhaps by a man driven by fear and desperation or by overwhelming anger.

Alfie sat back on his heels and inhaled the damp, sulphur-laden air. The cellar was full of London fog – you could almost taste the coal smoke from it.

It was not completely dark, though. Alfie began to look around and then he understood why the cellar was full of fog.

There was a faint gleam coming from the far side of the cellar. Alfie got to his feet and walked over. There was no need to feel his way. The light got stronger all the time: the white light of a gas lamp.

A gas lamp was shining into the cellar.

By the time Alfie reached the end wall, he realised where the light was coming from.

The cellar was very low. Its ceiling was only

inches above Alfie's head, so he was easily able to reach up and feel.

A square metal grid was set into the wall. Light and air poured through it. Was there any possibility that he could escape?

The metal plate was made up of squares about two inches across – only a rat could get through them – but if the plate itself could be removed, an opening of about sixteen inches would be left.

Alfie set to work.

Big Ben had struck the hour three times before Alfie gave up in despair. His nails and finger tops were bleeding and he was trembling in every limb. The lime plaster had crumbled away easily enough, but the metal plate had been well designed with bars inserted into the stone itself. There was no way that he could loosen it. He sank down on the ground and buried his head in his knees in despair.

It was at that moment that he heard a whisper.

For a moment he thought that he must have imagined it.

He had been half hoping that Richard might have followed him down to the cellar, might perhaps have got hold of the key. All the time that he had been working on the metal plate, Alfie had kept an ear open for sounds from the other side of the cellar.

But this whisper came from outside; from the place where the light and air flowed in.

In a moment Alfie was on his feet and stretching up to look out.

'Jack!' he said with disbelief.

And then, 'Mutsy!'

The big dog had his large, hairy face at the metal grid. Alfie passed a finger through to him and felt the gentle touch of a hot, rough tongue on his damaged fingertips. Then another face appeared beside the dog's. Jack was kneeling on the pavement and peering into the cellar. Alfie was weak with relief.

'Mutsy found you,' whispered Jack. 'We've been prowling around looking for you. Tom's here too. We were over by the Houses of Parliament when Mutsy started sniffing. You know the way he does . . . he dragged us across the road.'

'Can you get me out, Jack?' Alfie fought not to let shivers make his voice tremble.

Jack gave an experimental shake of the metal grid. 'Set fast, that is,' he muttered.

'Let me try.' Tom's face replaced his brother's, but

Alfie had no hope that the younger boy would succeed. Jack was a bit of a craftsman. He understood about buildings.

'Hang on a minute, Alfie.' Jack's face was back. 'I think you need an expert here. Lee the cracksman is the fella that you want. He owes me a favour. I'll just pop up to Duck Lane and be back in a couple of minutes.'

And then he was gone, leaving Tom and Mutsy behind. Alfie was glad of the company but wondered whether Jack should have taken Mutsy with him. Duck Lane was one of the worst streets in Devil's Acre. There were ten families to a room there, and every one of them destined for the hangman's noose, people used to say. It was not a safe place even in the middle of the day and, at night, it was one of the most dangerous places in London.

Still, Jack was well known all along the side of the River Thames and he had lots of strange friends. Even cracksmen knew that Jack would never betray their burglar activities to the police.

Alfie looked up at Tom.

'Sammy all right?' he asked in a whisper.

'Fine, a bit worried-like, but he said he knowed you'd turn up like a bad penny.' Tom was slightly uneasy with him, but, to Alfie, it seemed as though it was years since they had quarrelled. He had more serious things to think of now.

Like the fact that he was wanted for murder.

Jack was back soon with a man no bigger than himself. The man was wearing a broken bowler hat squashed down over his eyebrows and a black coat buttoned up high, covering his mouth and part of his nose. He said nothing to either Tom or Alfie; he just whispered instructions to Jack to keep watch with Mutsy. And then he kneeled down and immediately got out a small, gleaming hacksaw from one of his pockets and started to saw.

Metal against metal made a strange screaming noise and, from time to time, the cracksman stopped and looked all around. Jack was walking up and down with Mutsy and Tom was nervously going between them and the small slit into Alfie's cellar.

After a while the cracksman grunted with annoyance. He did not seem to be making much impression on the metal bar. He stopped working, turned slightly sideways until the light from the overhead gas lamp shone on him, then opened his coat and peered inside.

Where most people had silk linings to their coats, this cracksman had a hundred pockets, each one with a gleaming tool showing. Alfie watched with respect as the man ran his eyes along the rows and then selected a tiny file and carefully stowed away his little hacksaw.

Now the work progressed without pause. The small, razor-sharp file rubbed away at the bars until, first one, then two, then three and finally four were cut through and the metal panel was removed.

'Out,' the man said in a hoarse whisper to Alfie.

Alfie thrust his head through the gap, feeling a pair of horny hands grab him by the ears and unmercifully drag him up. For a moment he thought his head would come off, but then he angled his shoulders, let out his breath, and he was through.

'Let's get a bit of this stuff.' Lee searched again in one of his pockets and produced a sort of paste, well wrapped in a piece of oilcloth. Carefully he smeared the sawn edges of the metal and then pressed it back into place, holding it steadily for a few minutes.

'There you are then,' he whispered as he took his hand away. 'Good as new. No one will guess how the bird escaped from the cage.'

Alfie gave a quiet chuckle. 'There'll be stories about ghosts all over the school in the morning!' he said to Jack. 'Don't suppose that I will hear them, though,' he added. 'I'm not never going near the place again.'

CHAPTER 17

THE MYSTERIOUS SWEET

'I'm a bit puzzled and I need your help, Sammy, old son,' said Alfie, taking a place beside his blind younger brother. He had had a few hours' sleep and was beginning to feel much better. Soon it would be nine o'clock and Bow Street Police Station would be open. Alfie had decided to go straight to Inspector Denham, but there were a couple of things he wanted to clear up first.

'Anything that I can do?' asked Jack.

'Not really – it's a sort of brain thing.'

'I'll be off then and get another bit of coal before Tom is back,' said Jack cheerfully, showing no sign of taking offence at Alfie's words. He took up a folded sack from beside the fireplace, draped it around his shoulders against the cold and damp and moved off, whistling cheerfully.

'Spit it out,' commanded Sammy with a smile. He always enjoyed using his sharp wits. Alfie told him the story of the box of sweets and the slip of paper with the row of numbers.

'The thing I must do now,' Alfie said, 'is to find out what that message means. I'm sure it must be a message, but it's just a whole lot of numbers.'

'Numbers, eh, not words.' Sammy spoke thoughtfully and then a half smile came over his face.

'What was that sentence of yours? The sentence that you saw written down: *The quick brown fox jumps over the lazy dog.* See, I remember it. Sarah told you it was easy to remember, didn't she?'

'So?'

'You're the one that can read properly,' said Sammy impatiently. 'I only know my letters. Do you remember how Mr Elmore at the Ragged School taught me the alphabet with the letters made from clay? I remember him saying that *x* and *z* weren't used much.'

'But they're in the words: *fox* and *lazy*,' interrupted Alfie. 'Well . . .oh . . .'

'Ah, you're beginning to twig, now, aint' you?' said Sammy with satisfaction. 'Thought you couldn't be all that stupid!'

Alfie ignored that. He was beginning to understand. 'Twenty-six letters in the alphabet,' he said slowly. He thought hard for a moment, trying to picture the words in his mind's eye, counting on his fingers and muttering his ABC until he came to the end of the recitation. 'As far as I can tell,' he said excitedly, 'it seems like every letter of the alphabet is in that sentence. If you give a number to each one of the letters in that sentence then you can send a private message anytime you want to.'

'Safer than a message that has the number one for *A*, the number two for *B* and so on,' agreed Sammy.

'Let's have a try,' said Alfie. He took a pointed piece of coal from the rusty old bucket by the fireplace and began to mark out the letters on the stone flag of the hearth, putting a number in front of each letter.

1 T	8 K	15 O	22 O	29 L
2 H	9 B	16 X	23 V	30 A
3 E	10 R	17 J	24 E	31 Z
4 Q	11 O	18 U	25 R	32 Y
5 U	12 W	19 M	26 T	33 D
6 I	13 N	20 P	27 H	34 O
7 C	14 F	21 S	28 E	35 G

'Thirty-five letters, and there's only twenty-six in the alphabet,' he said in a disappointed tone. He looked down his list. 'The word *the* comes in twice, and some of the other letters are repeated as well.'

'That don't matter,' said Sammy calmly. 'Whoever made up the code had to make a sentence that would be easy to remember. It has a picture in it, that sentence. You see the fox and the lazy dog in your mind. Even I can imagine it.'

'Well, here are the numbers from that message,' said Alfie. He took the slip of paper that he had taken from the organist's room and began to read aloud: 'The first number is twenty – that's a *P*; the second number is 5 – that's a *U*; the third number is 1 and that is a *T*.'

'*Put*' said Sammy, his voice high with excitement.

'The next word is dead easy: it's just 123 so it must be *the*.' Alfie gave a low whistle.

'Read out the next numbers,' ordered Sammy.

'Six of them in this word: 9, 5, 29, 29, 3, 1. The first letter is a *B* . . .'

'And the second is a *U*,' put in Sammy. He had an extraordinary memory.

And the third and fourth are both *L*.'

'And the last one is a *T*,' guessed Sammy.

'*Bullet*,' said Alfie. He stared at Sammy, hardly able to believe his eyes. 'Remember what Inspector Denham said about the new kind of rifle that's been passed to the Russians,' he said in almost a whisper.

'That's what I was thinking. Just work out the rest of it quickly.' Sammy's face was flushed with excitement.

'*PUT THE BULLET INTO THE FUDGE*,' yelled Alfie triumphantly. 'And one of the sweets in the box is called *fudge* – Richard said so. Looks a squashy sort of one, too.' He picked up the box and smelled the sweet in the very centre of the rows, the one that Richard had pointed out was called fudge. This sweet did not have the same mouth-watering scent as the others: it smelled bitter. It looked powdery, too. Perhaps, he thought, you could dip the bullet into it and it would keep its shape even when the bullet was removed, like a sort of mould. He prodded it with his finger and nodded with satisfaction. Yes, it would be perfect for that.

At that very moment there was a knock at the door. His heart sank for a moment. It was probably the rent collector. He was not due today, but he did what he liked and his demands had to be met. Still, the knock didn't sound loud enough for him. Perhaps it was Inspector Denham or one of his constables. Alfie went to the door and opened it. A tall man, wearing a coat, hat and scarf, a man who smelled of cigars stood there, his right hand buried in his pocket.

'Alfie Sykes?' he asked. And then looked into the fire-lit cellar. 'And our property, the box of sweets; and the blind boy,' he said with satisfaction. 'Alfie, you come with me!' He spoke in strongly accented English. His left hand went to Alfie's collar. 'Come on, young man,' he said, still with that strong accent. 'You're coming with me, boy.'

And while his left arm grabbed the boy's wrist, his right hand aimed a gun directly at Sammy's heart.

CHAPTER 18

COURAGE

Sammy only heard the one short sentence: '*You're coming with me, boy.*' There were a few steps into the cellar, a gasp of pain from Alfie and a scuffling noise, and then footsteps – boots and bare feet, it sounded like – moving away.

The door slammed closed and Alfie was gone.

Left to himself, Sammy sat very still. One minute, he and Alfie were chatting, sharpening their wits on each other. And then he was alone.

Alfie had been dragged off.

The strange thing was that Alfie had not protested, had not shouted for help, had not tried to escape. He had gone with the rough-voiced stranger, gone without a word of protest.

There could only be one reason for that, thought Sammy, who knew Alfie well and knew the extent of his brother's courage.

Alfie had been threatened with a pistol and had gone with the man in order to avoid the two of them being shot here in the cellar below Bow Street.

Sammy sat very still and waited. There was no point in pursuit. Over the years Sammy had learned what he could do, and what was not possible for him. By the time he had managed to stumble out, there would have been no sign of Alfie and his captor. Even if he managed to get someone to go after them, the result would probably be a body – Alfie's – found in a dark doorway the following morning.

After a while, Sammy got up. Moving carefully, with outstretched hands, he made his way to the door. If only he had Mutsy, but the dog had gone with Tom for the breakfast sausages. The butcher was friendly and often gave Mutsy a bone, especially if he managed to catch a rat in the yard behind the shop.

Bow Street Police Station, thought Sammy, as he carefully crawled up the wet and slippery steps that led from the cellar to the level of the street.

Once he had reached the pavement, he clung with one hand to the iron railings which prevented pedestrians from falling from the street into the open area in front of the cellars and made his way slowly along, waiting for someone to offer to guide him.

'These children should be shut up in some institution,' muttered a woman as she passed him. His groping hand accidentally touched her dress and she shouted, 'Constable, can't you keep the streets clear for respectable women like myself?'

'You get on home, sonny,' said the constable's voice in Sammy's ear and Sammy turned his face in that direction and decided to trust the policeman. It sounded like PC 27.

'I have a message for Inspector Denham.' Sammy wished that he had not had to come out with these words in public. The trouble with being blind was that you never knew who might be listening. If only he could have had a quick look around, before speaking. The woman was still there; he sensed her anger.

'Could you take me to him?' He allowed a shake of

anxiety to come into his voice.

'All right, sonny,' said the constable. Sammy decided that it probably was PC 27. He was a decent fellow; Alfie always said that about this particular policeman.

Sammy leaned back gratefully as the constable put a large firm hand under Sammy's elbow. In another few minutes he would be with Inspector Denham and he would get help for his brother.

'I'll take him, Constable, if you wish?' Sammy listened anxiously to the voice. The accent was unusual. Was this man, also, a Russian? Another of the spies?

'That's all right, sir, I'm going that way myself.'

Sammy breathed a sigh of relief. But would the man be waiting for him on his return?

Still, at least he would have given the message to the inspector by then, and perhaps by then some police constable would be on Alfie's trail.

Inspector Denham greeted Sammy warmly, sent the constable for cakes and hot chocolate for both of them and settled down to hear what Sammy had to say. Sammy could hear the pen scratching across paper as he explained how he and Alfie worked out the code and Inspector Denham told him to slow down a few times.

'He's done well, your brother,' he said when he had heard the whole story. He spoke with a seriousness that Sammy appreciated. It struck him that Inspector Denham respected Alfie and was concerned about him, as though he had been someone important. 'Well, I've certainly got some good information for Scotland Yard.'

'Alfie wanted to get it all sorted out for you, sir,' said Sammy. 'He was wondering who had murdered the organist, the Russian spy, and why he was murdered in the yard outside the school. If you could get him back from the Russians – he's probably been taken to their Embassy – then he might be able to tell you the answer, sir.'

Inspector Denham sighed. 'The problem is, Sammy,' he said with a lowered voice, as though he did not wish any of the policemen in the outer office to hear him, 'the trouble is that if Alfie has got himself into the hands of the Russian Embassy, it's very difficult for us to rescue him. They have something called *diplomatic immunity* and that means that we cannot really send a party of policemen along to the

Russian Embassy and rescue your brother.'

'Does that mean that they can murder him, sir?' asked Sammy. He was amazed to find how calm his voice sounded.

'No,' said Inspector Denham and he spoke slowly and carefully. 'I don't think that they would go as far as that.'

He paused for a moment and then said, 'I don't know if you have ever played a game of chess, Sammy – I'd say that you and your brother could be good chess players – but I'll just explain to you what I'm going to do. If it were a game of chess, then they have made a move and now it's up to us to make the next move. What we'll do is this. We'll send a policeman, armed with a truncheon, to walk up and down Welbeck Street, opposite the Russian Embassy. I'll give the order straightaway. No one can object to that. He can chat to the nursemaids with children, keep an eye on the street hawkers, but . . . '

'But all the time,' Sammy broke in, 'if anyone looks out of the windows of the Russian Embassy, they will wonder what the policeman is doing and they will not want to have a body to dispose of . . . '

'Precisely,' said Inspector Denham, and there was

the hint of a smile in his voice. 'We'll keep a man on duty there, day and night, until your brother is back with you all in Bow Street. And for the moment, I will send my men around to Westminster School to work with the Scotland Yard crowd on the murder of Boris Ivanov and they will find out what's happening there.'

Inspector Denham's chair creaked and when he spoke again Sammy knew from his voice that the man had got to his feet. He took Sammy by the arm. 'Try not to worry too much. I promise you that I will get Alfie back for you as soon as possible. Here's a shilling for you; I'll put it into your pocket. Now the constable will see you home and make sure that one of the other lads has returned before he leaves you. And, Sammy, you stay there until we have news for you.'

He paused for a moment and said in a low voice, 'The streets of London are dangerous places for all of us, Sammy, sighted or not!'

CHAPTER 19

FLIGHT

Never argue with a man who holds a gun. Alfie couldn't remember who had said that to him, but it was good advice. He moved slightly ahead of the man with the gun, allowing his arm to be gripped tightly and never turning to try to see the face of his captor. It probably would have been of little use anyway. One quick glance in the cellar had shown him a tall black silk hat, a long black wool coat, and a white silk scarf wrapped around the lower half of the face and leaving nothing but a slit for the eyes between the brim of the hat and the folds of the scarf. Lots of Londoners dressed like that in these days of lung-choking fog.

Alfie had been born in the cellar at Bow Street and had lived there all of his life. Most of the people who lived thereabouts knew the four boys, but Alfie made no appeal for help as he passed up the street and then was escorted down Long Acre and towards Piccadilly Circus. The streets were crowded with people and the noise was deafening. The sound of a shot would be lost in the hullabaloo and the man could easily slip away.

But Alfie had not given up. Every fibre of his being was alert for an opportunity. He hoped desperately that some stranger might stop and ask the way of his captor. Two seconds' distraction would give him the chance to get away from the man with the gun. Already he sensed that the grip on his arm was not quite so firm.

Now they were going down Piccadilly. This was a street where all the toffs shopped or went to their clubs. The pair was beginning to attract more attention here. Not many bare-footed begging boys dared come down Piccadilly: policemen were everywhere.

'I say, ole man, whash he done?' The man asking

the question was quite drunk and his words slurred into one another. He stood right in front of the man with the gun, barring his way. 'Steal something, di' he?' he asked. 'I say, Constable, young scoundrel here . . . my fren . . . ' His voice was loud and a policeman turned and began to come across to them. The Russian hesitated and his hand on Alfie's arm slackened slightly.

Now or never! The words flashed through Alfie's mind and he sprang into action. He jabbed an elbow with all his force into the prominent stomach of the man holding him. There was a gasp of pain and suddenly the small, round, hard mouth of the pistol no longer pressed against the boy's spine.

Alfie took a chance. With a second jab of the elbow, he was off, running and dodging down the wide pavement of Piccadilly, past the big bookshop, past the fancy grocery shop.

'Shhtop thief!' The drunken man was laughing heartily but his cry was taken up. This was a respectable street. No one wanted ragged boys, probably picking the pockets of the rich, in a place like that.

Alfie ran past the doorway to Fortnum & Mason,

smelling the delicious smell of dried fruit wafting from the shop. For a moment he wondered whether to turn down the small street beside it, but there was a big delivery van there and the place swarmed with shop assistants unloading supplies. Any one of those could trip him up and claim a reward.

And then he remembered that Green Park must not be too far away. If he could get a start on his pursuers then he might be able to hide in one of the bushes there, or even better, climb a tree and hide there until the hunt was given up.

He dodged behind a man opening his umbrella then sprinted ahead and turned into Green Park

On a foggy, cold day like this day, Green Park should have been empty.

But it wasn't!

It was jammed with people – men, women and children. Some were standing on the grass beneath the trees, some on the paths, and all of them were looking upwards.

And there, in the centre of the park, high above the trees, straining its ropes was a giant, brightly-coloured hot-air balloon, made from strips of yellow and red silk.

The balloon was the shape of a giant egg, with the patterned silk stretched over a wire framework. Dangling from beneath the egg shape was a basket made from bamboo.

Alfie pushed his way into the centre of the crowd, using his knees and elbows. He would get as far from the man with the gun as he could. After a few minutes, he managed to get himself a place just beside the balloon. No one could touch him here, he thought as he cast a quick look over his shoulder. There were a lot of heavily-built men around, carrying up bags of sand and handing them into the swaying basket. A warmly dressed man in a fur cap stood there. The balloonist, no doubt, thought Alfie.

'More!' shouted one of the men. 'We need more ballast. This basket will turn over if we don't have a bit more weight in it.'

'One more bag to go,' grunted one of carriers. 'It weighs about five stone.'

'Should be enough,' replied the balloonist. 'Hurry up. We must get going. We're five minutes overdue already. Fling it over, man.'

Perhaps the man was rushed or perhaps the bag already had a split in it, but as he flung it through the air a stream of sand fell straight down and powdered the grass. By the time the balloonist caught it, the bag had less than half of its contents left.

'Look what you've done, you awkward fool!' shouted the balloonist. 'I can't go up without that last bag of sand. Look at the basket!'

There was no doubt that the basket was not properly weighted down. The ropes were slack and the basket swung to one side and then tilted to the other. Even Alfie could see that those ropes needed to be stretched taut, like the balloons that he had seen from time to time floating across the London sky.

Alfie had only survived the life of a street boy in London by having quick wits and plenty of courage. In a second he had made up his mind and a second later he was inside the bamboo basket, sitting on the floor with his arms around his knees.

'Take me,' he said. 'I weigh exactly five stone.'

Alfie didn't have a notion of what he weighed, but he had seen large machines inside chemists' shops and was ready to swear to how, when and why he had been weighed on one of them.

The balloonist, however, took one glance at the boy

and made up his mind. If Alfie had been a well-dressed, well-fed young gentleman he would not have risked it, but a ragged slum child was a different matter. No one would worry about him.

'Cast off!' he shouted.

Instantly the men holding the ropes let go. The gleaming silk swelled and surged, the pointed top rising towards the sky.

'Hold on tight to that rope. Don't wriggle and, whatever you do, don't stand up!' said the balloonist sternly.

Alfie was only too glad to stay still and to keep his head down. He wondered whether the man who was chasing him had seen him get into the balloon. Well, if he had, there wasn't much that he could do about it now!

Peering through the cracks in the woven cane of the basket, Alfie was surprised to find that he was staring at the roof of one of the clubs beside Green Park. Already that high! Where was the man going, he wondered but didn't bother to ask. The balloonist was on his feet now, tugging at a red cord that seemed to be attached to a sort of flap at the top of the balloon.

'Need to get a bit more height,' he yelled when he

saw Alfie looking at him. 'I forgot about that huge plane tree over here. Should have avoided it.'

The next minute the basket hit the tree. A few crows squawked, rose indignantly up into the air and flew away. Alfie shut his eyes and then opened them. The cane basket was stuck, like a giant nest, but it was undamaged. The enormous silk balloon was still full of hot air and it rose above the branches and tugged at the ropes like a living creature. The balloonist pulled once more on the red cord.

'There we go!' the balloonist exclaimed as the balloon gave one last tug and the basket floated free. Alfie heard a cheer from the crowd below. The basket was rising rapidly.

We must be well above the tops of the houses now, he thought and peered over the side of the basket, taking care not to move his position.

'Well,' he said aloud. 'I ain't never seen London look like that before.'

Suddenly the city that he knew so well looked like a picture. Down below him were towers, churches, domed buildings, smoking chimneys, houses the size of a large dog, tiny ships floating on a silver river crossed by toy bridges. He spotted the spire of St

Martin's church and the fountains of Trafalgar Square. He looked east and thought he glimpsed the stately pillars in front of the Covent Garden Theatre and the crowded streets around the market. He strained his eyes to try to make out Bow Street and that made him think of Sammy and how his brother had been left alone when he, Alfie, had been taken from the cellar at the point of a gun. He wondered what Sammy had done. Would he have guessed what was going on?

Alfie forced his mind away from Sammy; there was nothing he could do and his brother usually found his way out of trouble. He looked up and saw the veils of fog were touched with gold, like a silk lining to a grey coat.

'Cor,' he said. 'I never knowed that the sun stayed up there all the time behind the fog!' And then he thought that sounded a bit childish and said in a business-like tone, 'Where are you bound, Mister?'

'Vauxhall Gardens,' said the balloonist. 'I'm going to give rides in the balloon there tonight. There's going to be a firework display and I'll take people up for half a crown so that they can see the sights. You enjoying yourself?'

'How far is that from Westminster?' asked Alfie,

wondering how he was going to get back. He had often heard of Vauxhall Gardens, of course. People who had money went there to amuse themselves, but Alfie had never had money to waste on things like that. Money was for the rent and for food and that was all it could be used for in Alfie's life.

'About a mile beside the river,' said the man. 'Look down; we're nearly there.'

Alfie peered over the edge again. They were drifting along the line of the river high above the ships and boats.

'Lambeth Bridge,' said the man, pointing. 'Look, Vauxhall Gardens are there. They cost a shilling to get into, sixpence for children, but you're in luck. You'll get in free because you're with me. Hang on tight, now. This is where we go down.'

The balloonist hauled on the red cord which led upwards into the balloon. The vent for the hot air widened dramatically and the balloon began to sink. Suddenly the ground seemed to rush up to meet them. The basket bumped along the grass, dragged by the half-deflated silken mass of the balloon.

'We're here!' shouted the balloonist. 'Hop out like a good lad and hang onto the rope with all your strength. Don't let it go, whatever you do.'

Alfie did as he was told. He wrapped the rope around his waist for double security, and looked up.

And looked straight into the eyes of the man with the gun.

CHAPTER 20

SHUFFLEBOTTOM

In a flash, Alfie understood what had happened. The man with the gun must have seen him go up in the balloon, found out where it was heading and taken a cab to Vauxhall Gardens.

Instantly Alfie hopped back into the basket.

'Need any help, Mister?' he asked. 'Anything you want doing? It'll save you getting more sand.'

'No, it won't,' said the balloonist. 'I'd be dumping a couple of bags now. I'll be taking up passengers soon.' He looked at Alfie. 'Anything the matter?' he asked.

'Just a man with a gun after me,' said Alfie, trying to sound tough.

'That's a nuisance,' said the balloonist absent-mindedly, fiddling with the cords coming from the valve. 'And you don't have a gun, right?'

'Right,' said Alfie, wondering if the man was mad.

'And you want to get away? Quite right, too. I'd do the same in your place. Frankie!' He shouted the last word and a man in the blue and white uniform of a waterman came forward.

'Frankie, take this lad back to Westminster, will you? Did me a favour. Game lad, plenty of courage. Never batted an eye when we went into a tree. He's a bit worried about a man with a gun after him, though. And who could blame him?'

The balloonist was in good humour. A long queue of people to buy tickets to go up in the balloon was forming.

Alfie took one look at the man called Frankie. He looked tough and Alfie decided to trust this stranger. He clambered out of the basket and took his place beside the waterman.

He looked behind him a few times as they walked together through the crowds, but the man with the gun was keeping well out of sight. My lucky day, thought Alfie and said no more until he was in the wide, low boat moored beside the Vauxhall Steps.

'Westminster?' asked Frankie with a lift of an eyebrow.

'Westminster,' repeated Alfie in a loud, clear tone of voice. Let the man with the gun take a cab and be waiting at Westminster Steps. Alfie had another trick up his sleeve.

'Temple Stairs suit you as well?' he asked quietly as Frankie pulled strongly on the oars and set the boat on its course right down the centre of the River Thames.

'You didn't say that back there.' Frankie made the observation but he continued to pull strongly against the oncoming tide and his broad, placid face was unchanged.

'Don't ever say where you're going when there's a man with a gun around,' said Alfie. His voice, to his pleasure, sounded calm and unworried.

'Puts you off, don't it, having a gun pointed at you,' agreed Frankie. He drove his oars deeply into the water and made the boat leap forward before saying, 'What's he after you for, then?'

'Police business,' said Alfie, looking directly into the waterman's face.

'Won't meddle in it, then,' said Frankie. He was silent for a moment before saying, 'You should get yourself a gun.'

'Should, indeed,' said Alfie grandly. 'I've been taking shooting lessons at a place near Leicester Square,' he added. 'Don't know if you've heard of it. Called George's Shooting Gallery.'

'Good fellow, George,' said Frankie. 'Know him well.'

'Good fellow,' agreed Alfie. 'You take lessons from him, then?'

Frankie gave a grunt. 'You must be joking,' he said. 'Where would I get the money for something like that?' He steered expertly around a dredging barge and said nothing for a moment or two and then resumed.

'Naw, sometimes I row some toffs to Hungerford Steps and that's where they're bound. George gives me a shilling if I send a customer to him. Straight as a die is George. Sent him a man last Friday night. And there he was, Saturday morning, punctual as a clerk to his desk, shilling in his hand. Nice fellow, George. A lot of others would have pretended that the man never arrived.'

'Stays open late, then, does he; George, I mean?' enquired Alfie, in an off-hand way.

'As late as it takes,' confirmed Frankie. 'It must have been about eleven o'clock of the evening when I dropped off this fellow.'

Not very likely then, thought Alfie, that George had anything to do with the death of Boris, the Russian spy. No, it must be Ron Shufflebottom that was responsible for the death of Boris Ivanov. Or was there another possibility? Alfie sat very still as ideas darted through his head.

'So why are they after you, then?' asked Frankie, looking at him shrewdly. 'A man with a gun? Why should anyone bother about you?'

'Wish I never got myself tangled in this business,' groaned Alfie, avoiding the question.

'What business?' The waterman was gazing at him with interest.

'Any chance you were around Westminster Steps on Friday evening?' Alfie asked the question with little hope in his voice and was not surprised when the man shook his head.

'Naw,' he said. 'Not much business around Westminster in the evening. The cabmen have it all sewn up. But, now that I come to think of it, I did get a fare on Friday – early Friday evening – going to Westminster. Crowd of drunken Yorkshire men. They'd come two hundred miles to London to hear their Member of Parliament speak in a debate about a new law saying that children under nine could only work for twelve hours a day. All mill owners, they were, and said that they could never make a living if the new law was brought in. They was hoping that their Member of Parliament would speak up for them.'

'What was his name?' asked Alfie.

Frankie chuckled. 'Not a name that you could forget. Shufflebottom! What a name, eh?' His laugh rumbled out.

Alfie laughed too but he was thinking furiously. If the mill owners had come all the way from Yorkshire to hear Ron Shufflebottom argue about how long children should work – well, then, there was no chance that he could have left the Houses of Parliament early.

No, thought Alfie, his heart sinking, Ron

Shufflebottom was not responsible for the death of Boris Ivanov on Friday night. He had begun to guess what had happened on that night.

'Well, here we are at Temple Stairs,' said Frankie, interrupting his thoughts. 'Mind how you go. Remember what I said. Get yourself a gun and some lessons. London is a very dangerous place.'

CHAPTER 21

BLACKMAIL

'Thought I'd find you here.' Alfie used the knee of an angel as a foothold and grabbed its arm to lever himself up beside Richard. The moon was waning, but the night was clear with a hint of frost whitening the roofs and exposing a sky brilliant with stars.

Alfie sat for a moment looking down on the boats on the river and at the gas lamps lining the streets. The windows of the Houses of Parliament were all dark. The Members of Parliament were spending the weekend with their families all over the country.

Richard gave him a sidelong glance. 'You, again,' he said. 'So you're still around.'

'Me, again,' agreed Alfie cheerfully. And then, he asked, 'Why do you come up here so often? Don't you get tired of it? What do you think about when you're up here on your own?'

Richard didn't answer for a moment; he just turned his head slowly, gazing down at the miles of London spread beneath them.

'I think about money,' he said unexpectedly. 'You know, London is the richest city in the world. My father told me that and he's a banker. If you half shut your eyes all the lights down there look like piles of gold. And I think that someday I'll own them all. But you wouldn't understand,' he added, and there was a note of contempt in his voice.

'So your father is a banker,' said Alfie mildly. 'Brought you up to the money trade, is that it?'

Richard smiled. 'My mother used to tell me that ten minutes after I was born my father put a gold sovereign into my hand and I grabbed it tightly. He was very proud of me, that's what she used to say.'

'Used to . . .' hinted Alfie.

'She's dead, now,' said Richard, turning his face

away again and once more looking down on the rich city of London.

'My father will take me into partnership when I've left finished my studies. He wants me to go to Oxford, but I'd like to go straight into the City and begin making my fortune.' His voice sounded impatient.

Alfie looked down, too.

Funny old place, London, he thought with surprise. He would never have guessed that it was the richest city in the world. Anyone who thought that had never been down the streets of Devil's Acre or wandered around St Giles. Not much richness there.

He turned his attention back to Richard. 'So you don't want to wait till you leave school, that's it, is it?' he asked casually. 'Gone into business on your own, while you're waiting, like.'

Richard opened his mouth and then shut it.

'The blackmail business – that was it, wasn't it?'

And that was it, Alfie thought sadly. An easy way of making money – blackmail. You got hold of someone with a secret and threatened to tell the secret unless they gave you money to keep silent. Richard had not been helping him just for a lark, as he had thought. Richard must have been using information from Alfie in order to blackmail the Russian organist. Richard would have threatened Boris that he would tell everyone that the organist was giving British secrets to the Russians.

Boris would have been desperate. He wouldn't have wanted to go to prison. He probably wanted to keep his job at Westminster Abbey. He might have loved his job, thought Alfie, remembering the organ notes that had streamed out from the church into the winter's air.

'Why did you kill him?' he asked casually.

'I didn't!' There was a note of alarm in Richard's voice. And something else, too. Something that made Alfie brace himself and grab the tight curls on the angel's head.

'How could I have the strength or the height to do that?' Richard moved a little closer and eyed Alfie's clenched hand. 'You know yourself that someone broke off the flagpole and hit him over the head with it,' he added. 'The police say that it had to be a very tall and very strong man who did it.'

'That's what the police from Scotland Yard say? Is that right?' enquired Alfie with a tolerant chuckle. 'Not too bright, are they?'

'What do you mean?' Richard moved a little closer still.

'Stay right where you are.' Alfie kept his voice friendly as he went on, 'I got a gun here in my jacket pocket. I've been taking a few lessons from George at the shooting gallery. Won a bet from him and he gave me this old pistol.'

It was pure bluff; but Richard, he was glad to see, had hesitated. He couldn't take the chance, thought Alfie as he poked his finger through the threadbare material of his coat, hoping that it looked like the barrel of a gun.

'Go on then, tell me how I could possibly kill Boris,' challenged Richard.

'You pushed him off the roof, of course, and he hit his head against the flagpole, breaking it off as he fell. I saw straightaway that was how it happened,' boasted Alfie.

'And why should I kill Boris? What was he doing on the roof in the first place?'

'I've been thinking about that,' said Alfie calmly. 'I'd say this is what happened. You passed him a note, after choir practice probably, and asked him whether he wanted to sample some sweets that you had in your room. He came, of course; you knew that he would. When he was there you showed him a small box, the same size as the one we took from his room, all wrapped in brown paper. Poor old Boris would have been shocked that anyone knew about these sweets and how he was spying for the Russians. You said that you would give it back to him if he paid the price. Then you took the money and, before he could do anything, you shoved the box out of the window. It slid down the roof into the yard. I saw it myself when I saw the body – nearly skidded on it.

'The body, ah,' said Richard suavely. His eyes were on the baggy pocket in the torn jacket and Alfie moved his hand slightly, making sure that his finger was poking out stiffly through the jacket like the barrel of a gun.

'Boris must've gone onto the roof to get the box back . . . I guess it didn't fall into the yard straightaway,' Alfie continued. 'Once he was out there, you gave him a push. I suppose he'd threatened to tell your father, the banker, about the interesting way that his son was making money. I don't suppose that he was the first person you've blackmailed.'

'You can't prove anything,' said Richard. He gave a

yawn, but his face in the starlight looked very white. 'No one would believe you.'

'I could put the idea into the heads of some of them dumb policemen from Scotland Yard, though, couldn't I?' Alfie's voice hardened. 'There'd be questions. Things would come to light.'

There was a long silence and then Richard said abruptly, 'It was an accident. I didn't mean to kill him.'

'Thought he would bounce, did you?' asked Alfie with a smile.

'Anyway, I don't see why you care – he was a spy, wasn't he? I did it for my country.'

'Ah, but you went a bit further, didn't you?' Alfie replied in the same calm tone of voice. 'You went to the Russian Embassy and told them that I had the box. You didn't want any chance of them being after you. They might have been a bit too much for you to handle. So you sent them to me.'

'Might one enquire how you know this?' Richard had a sneering note to his voice, but his eyes were sharp and he shifted his position to just a little nearer to Alfie.

'They knew what my name was and where I lived, and about my brother being blind and about me having the box,' answered Alfie promptly. 'You told them to aim at Sammy, didn't you? You'd have been glad to have him killed, wouldn't you? Jealous that he had a better voice than you, I wouldn't be surprised.'

'You're talking nonsense,' said Richard in a lofty tone. 'But I'm sorry for you. Living in that terrible place and wearing those awful dirty clothes and having a blind brother. So I'm going to give you a little present, if you swear never to say anything about this to any living creature for the whole of your life.' He reached into his pocket, took out a folding purse and opened it. Alfie gasped. It was full of sovereigns and at the back were folded bank notes. One of them was a twenty-pound note.

'I can see that your father is going to be very, very proud of you,' Alfie said sarcastically.

'Here you are,' said Richard. 'What will it take? One sovereign? Two . . .'

Alfie hesitated but not for long. He had been to see Inspector Denham that morning. The five pounds was safely stashed away in the rent box and in his pocket were five silver shillings sent down by Scotland Yard and delivered to the cellar by PC 27. He took a deep breath and looked Richard steadily in the eye.

'I'd rather have nothing more to do with you, or your money,' he said. 'But you don't need to worry. I'm not bringing this story to the police. I've done my job and you did help – and I believe you when you say you didn't mean to kill. Just a spot of blackmail.'

Richard's eyes flickered. He shrugged his shoulders. 'Better be going,' he said uncertainly.

Alfie gestured towards the parapet. There was no way he was going first. He didn't trust Richard. 'After you, sir,' he said.

CHAPTER 22

THE GANG

Alfie looked around the cellar. The task was over and the spies had been uncovered. Inspector Denham had told Alfie that Ron Shufflebottom had been arrested for passing secrets to the Russians. Apparently he had confessed very quickly. The reward had been claimed and the gang were safe from the rent collector and would have a roof over their heads for the months to come.

And yet, there was something wrong.

There wasn't the same air of excitement, the same

sense of achievement as at the other times they had solved mysteries. Alfie thought that he knew why. For once it was not a solution that the gang had worked together to produce.

Alfie had gone out on his own – gone with a strange boy – with Richard Green from Westminster School. Alfie winced. He did not want to think of Richard and he turned his mind to when he had floated over London in a balloon.

That was it. An idea seemed to float from the balloon into his mind and once more he counted out the money in his pocket.

'It's your half-day, Sarah,' he said. 'Let's treat ourselves to an evening out at Vauxhall Gardens.'

Frankie was at the Temple Stairs with his boat when the five of them trooped down, followed by Mutsy.

'Here, I don't take dogs,' said Frankie as they approached.

'Very good guard dog; better than any gun; available free of charge to any obliging waterman,' said Alfie smartly.

'He's really good at catching rats, too, if you want your mooring place cleared,' put in Jack.

'Go on, get in,' said Frankie. 'Keep him still. Where are you off to?'

'Vauxhall Gardens' said Alfie grandly.

'I'll pay half; I got some good tips from customers last night,' said Sarah in a low voice when they reached the gardens, and Alfie allowed her. This would leave money for a slap-up supper.

It was beginning to get dark when they arrived and Vauxhall Gardens, all decked out ready for Christmas, was a wonderful sight. The trees and colonnades that lined the paths were strung with two thousand coloured lamps and in the background there was a sudden flash as fireworks sped up into the sky. Mutsy stared in astonishment and had to be prevented by Tom from howling with amazement.

'They're like a huge wheel,' Alfie explained to Sammy. 'They're like gold lines coming out from the centre and whirling around. I've never seen anything like it!' He struggled for words, trying to explain this tremendous sight to his brother.

You have to be your brother's eyes, his grandfather had said to Alfie when he was quite young. *Don't ever let him be wondering what everyone is looking at; tell him.*

'And now it's turning different colours! It's green and yellow and red!'

'What's that?' Sammy's ear was turned towards a large circular building. The sounds of musical instruments were coming from there.

'Listen!' Sammy seized his arm and Alfie listened. 'They're playing firework music,' said Sammy in a hushed voice. 'Go on telling me about the fireworks, but quiet-like. I want to listen. They're playing it like I imagine the fireworks look.'

So Alfie went on describing the fireworks, how some of them blossomed into pink and yellow flowers, like the ones that grew in the public parks, and how others flew through the air like birds of paradise. Sammy sighed with pleasure and didn't move until the last notes of the orchestra faded into silence. Even Mutsy stayed very still, his large intelligent eyes fixed on Sammy as though he understood that this was something very important for one of his masters.

'Everything is free here,' said Tom, appearing beside them. 'You can do anything you like and it's all free! Let's go and see the cascade.'

The cascade was magnificent. It was like a wall of water pouring down continuously, working miniature watermills and flowing into a river which disappeared behind the stage with small ships sailing on it.

'Supper,' said Alfie, once he had dragged Tom out from the building where he was investigating a large pump in the company of Mutsy.

'It's so beautiful,' said Sarah, looking around the restaurant once they were seated and eyeing the walls covered in enormous mirrors. 'Look how the coloured lights are reflected by these. I think I'll have a word with the landlord at the White Horse Inn. Something like this would be a great attraction in his supper room. He and I have great plans for that new room.'

'Supper, Miss?' The waiter addressed himself to Sarah as the most respectable one of the group.

'What shall we have?' Sarah looked around at the gang. Mutsy, a dog of discretion, had hidden himself beneath the table and only the tip of his hairy tail appeared from under the long skirt of the tablecloth.

'Beg pardon, Miss, if I could suggest. The chicken is very good, Miss, cooked at the table in front of your eyes. Glass of wine, Miss?'

'Beer,' decided Sarah. She looked around at the nodding heads, 'And, yes, the chicken sounds good.'

* * *

'Melts in the mouth, this stuff,' said Jack approvingly.

'Mutsy likes it; his tail is whipping my ankles,' said Tom with his mouth full.

Alfie had never tasted chicken before in his life and the creamy softness of its velvet-like texture was something that he thought he would never forget. More and more dishes of different vegetables and sauces were brought and even Tom found it hard to finish what was on his plate.

'What will we do now?' asked Sarah. 'I'd love to go up on that swinging boat, Jack, if you'd come with me.'

'I want to have another look at that thing that pumps the cascade,' said Tom. 'Come on, Mutsy, old boy. Rats! If you catch one, the man in charge might let me have a look at how they made the watermill.'

Alfie looked at Sammy. He rather fancied having a go on the swinging boat himself, and he knew that Sammy would enjoy it.

But there was something else that Sammy would enjoy more; Alfie realised that.

'Let's go over to the Rotunda,' he said. 'There's a concert starting there in ten minutes.'

The Rotunda was a beautifully decorated place,

built in a circle with a stage in the middle of it. It was covered in paintings – Chinese, Alfie heard someone say. It was the second performance of the evening so they got good seats, right near the stage, and Sammy was rigid with excitement from the moment that the players began to tune their instruments.

'It's Handel's *Water Music*,' Alfie whispered in his ear and Sammy nodded.

Poor Sammy, thought Alfie. He could almost feel the waves of longing coming from his brother as his hands moved softly in time to the music. If only their grandfather's fiddle had not been sold. It was one of the first things that Sammy and Alfie's mother had done after her father's death. Alfie thought of Richard and money and how much he would like to get music lessons for Sammy, and to buy one of those gleaming stringed instruments that the men on the stage handled with such care. Blindness would not matter to a player in an orchestra.

Eventually the music finished and everyone began to move outside, talking and laughing. Sammy sat very still and Alfie stayed beside him. 'What are you thinking about?' asked Sammy after a minute.

'I was thinking about Richard,' said Alfie. Sammy

was the only one that he had told the whole story to.

'Poor old Richard,' said Sammy compassionately. 'I'm sorry for him, really.'

Alfie turned surprised eyes on him. 'Sorry for Richard?' he asked. 'Why?'

Sammy shrugged. 'Got no family, no gang . . . On his own most of the time . . . I wouldn't like to be him,' he said. 'We have a good time, don't we? Us and Mutsy – and having treats like this.'

Alfie squeezed his arm. 'I suppose you're right, old son,' he said. 'Richard has pots of money, but he don't seem none too happy.' He spoke lightly, but he knew what Sammy meant. He and his gang would survive; Alfie was certain of that. And who knows, he thought, what we might do in the years to come.

ACKNOWLEDGEMENTS

Thanks are due to Anne Clark and the team at Piccadilly who have spared no efforts to make the book as perfect as it can be, to Peter Buckman of Ampersand Agency, who always finds time to read and comment on my many books, and to my family and friends who have to put up with me when I get lost in the fogs of Victorian London.

This is the sixth 'Alfie' book and once again I must acknowledge my debt of gratitude to the man who was my inspiration for the series. I first read the novels of Charles Dickens when I was seven and, throughout a sickly and bed-ridden childhood, I devoured every one of them – and then re-read them until even now I can identify almost every line. I regard Dickens as the greatest novelist that England has produced and I hope that young people who enjoy the *London Murder Mysteries* may go on to read his wonderful stories.

THE MONTGOMERY MURDER

The police must move fast to catch the killer of wealthy Mr Montgomery. They need an insider, someone streetwise, cunning, bold . . . someone like Alfie. When Inspector Denham makes him an offer, Alfie and his gang must sift clues, shadow suspects and negotiate a sinister world of double-dealing and danger.

THE DEADLY FIRE

A man's body lies in the burnt-out wreckage of the Ragged School.
The police say the fire was just an accident –
but Alfie suspects foul play.
Determined to find out the truth, Alfie and his gang must follow up each clue, investigate every suspect and risk their lives on the dangerous streets of Victorian London – until the ruthless murderer is caught.

MURDER ON STAGE

A scream rings out through the theatre. The man on
stage is dead! Who killed him? Alfie has a few suspects
in his sights. But when the spotlight turns on
Alfie himself, the search for the murderer becomes
a fight for his own survival.

DEATH OF A CHIMNEY SWEEP

Alfie knew who it was the moment he saw the body
under the gas lamp. Joe the chimney sweep.
No one else seems to care about the death of a poor
boy, but Alfie has reason to believe that Joe was
murdered. So he and his gang will risk their lives on
the rooftops of London and brave the dark,
dangerous world of the chimney sweeps, until they
uncover the deadly truth.

The London Murder Mysteries

The BODY
IN FOG
THE

The body lies beneath a statue in Trafalgar Square.

Alfie and his gang set out to find the murderer, just
as a thick fog turns the London streets into a sinister
maze. But soon Alfie is plunged into a still more
terrifying world hidden below the city . . .

Praise for *The London Murder Mysteries*:

'Fast-paced . . . excellent.'
parentsintouch

*'Fast-moving . . . gruesome . . .
wonderful descriptions.'*
School Librarian

THE LONDON MURDER MYSTERIES

www.piccadillypress.co.uk/
londonmurdermysteries

Head online to find out more
about Alfie's world!

SAXBY SMART
PRIVATE DETECTIVE
SIMON CHESHIRE

Be the sleuth yourself and crack all the cases!

In each story Saxby Smart – schoolboy detective – gives you, the reader, clues which help solve the mystery. Are you 'smart' enough to find the answers?

The **Curse** of the **Ancient Mask**

A mysterious curse, suspicious sabotage of a school competition, and a very unpleasant relative all conspire to puzzle Saxby Smart, schoolboy private detective.

Stories include: *The Curse of the Ancient Mask*, *The Mark of the Purple Homework* and *The Clasp of Doom*.

The Hangman's Lair

A terrifying visit to the Hangman's Lair to recover stolen money, a serious threat of blackmail, and a mystery surrounding a stranger's unearthly powers test Saxby to the limit in this set of case files!

Stories include: *The Hangman's Lair*, *Diary of Fear* and *Whispers from the Dead*.

www.saxbysmart.co.uk

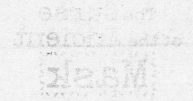